Holocaust Deniers and Conspiracy Theorists

Other Books in the Current Controversies Series

Agriculture
America's Mental Health Crisis
The Dark Web
Domestic vs. Offshore Manufacturing
Environmental Catastrophe
Fair Trade
Freedom of the Press
The Gig Economy
Immigration, Asylum, and Sanctuary Cities
Medical Use of Illicit Drugs
Nativism, Nationalism, and Patriotism

Holocaust Deniers and Conspiracy Theorists

Bridey Heing, Book Editor

Published in 2021 by Greenhaven Publishing, LLC
353 3rd Avenue, Suite 255, New York, NY 10010

Copyright © 2021 by Greenhaven Publishing, LLC

First Edition

All rights reserved. No part of this book may be reproduced in any form without permission in writing from the publisher, except by a reviewer.

Articles in Greenhaven Publishing anthologies are often edited for length to meet page requirements. In addition, original titles of these works are changed to clearly present the main thesis and to explicitly indicate the author's opinion. Every effort is made to ensure that Greenhaven Publishing accurately reflects the original intent of the authors. Every effort has been made to trace the owners of the copyrighted material.

Cover image: James Leynse/Getty Images

Library of Congress Cataloging-in-Publication Data

Names: Heing, Bridey, editor.
Title: Holocaust deniers and conspiracy theorists / Bridey Heing, book
   éditor.
Description: First edition. | New York : Greenhaven Publishing, 2021. |
   Series: Current controversies | Includes bibliographical references and
   index. | Audience: Grades 9–12.
Identifiers: LCCN 2019058831 | ISBN 9781534507036 (library binding) | ISBN
   9781534507029 (paperback)
Subjects: LCSH: Conspiracy theories—Juvenile literature. | Holocaust
   denial—Juvenile literature.
Classification: LCC HV6275 .H65 2021 | DDC 001.9—dc23
LC record available at https://lccn.loc.gov/2019058831

Manufactured in the United States of America

Website: http://greenhavenpublishing.com

Contents

Foreword   11

Introduction   14

Chapter 1: Are Conspiracy Theories Dangerous?

Overview: Conspiracy Theories Have Long Been Part of American Public Discourse   18

Liberty Vittert

Although conspiracy theories seem to be on the rise, they have in fact been common in American public debate for at least a century. Some have been dangerous while others have been benign.

Yes: Conspiracy Theories Can Encourage Violence or Other Harmful Actions

Law Enforcement Indicates That Conspiracy Theories Can Be Directly Linked to Extremism   21

Jason Wilson

A report by the FBI suggests that conspiracy theories can feed into extremist views and violence, making them a potential threat to public safety.

Reports Indicate a Connection Between Conspiracy Theories and Domestic Terrorism   24

Luke Barnes

If driven to action, conspiracy theorists could become domestic terrorists, according to law enforcement.

Conspiracy Theories Change How Some People Behave in Dangerous Ways   28

Timothy Callaghan and Matt Motta

Parents put their children and other children at risk due to conspiracy theories about vaccines, which have led to a rise in rates of preventable and formerly eradicated diseases, like measles.

Conspiracy Theories Spread Quickly, Sow Doubt, and Dehumanize the Victims of Tragedies   33

The Information Disorder Lab Team

Fringe websites and social media users have circulated the term "crisis actor" to dismiss crisis victims and assert that events were faked for political gain. This has negative effects on victims as well as those who believe these fast-spreading conspiracy theories.

No: Conspiracy Theories Are Harmless Beliefs That Have No Impact on the Real World

People with Certain Psychological Traits Are Likely to Believe in Conspiracy Theories   37

Joshua Hart

Conspiracy theories are most appealing to people who fit a particular psychological profile, not those with underlying potentially threatening characteristics.

Conspiracy Theories Are Not Harmful by Nature and Can Even Hold Those in Power Accountable   41

Daniel Cohnitz

Although some conspiracy theories may pose a threat to public safety, conspiracy theories in general are not inherently a threat to society.

Conspiracy Theorists Can See Reason   49

Mark Lorch

Understanding why people believe conspiracy theories can allow us to find ways to counter those beliefs and may even convince some that a conspiracy theory is not true.

Chapter 2: Does the Internet Spread Conspiracy Theories?

Overview: The Internet Interacts with Conspiracy Theories in Unique Ways   57

Joe Uscinski

While conspiracy theories predate the internet, communication on the internet has allowed them to spread quicker. However, this does not necessarily mean that engagement with conspiracy theories has changed significantly as a result.

Yes: Twitter and Other Websites Have Allowed Conspiracy Theories to Flourish

The Internet Is Making It Possible for Falsehoods to Spread Quicker Than Ever Before   62
David Dunning
Misinformation, which can include conspiracy theories, spreads quickly on the internet, and people are not always good at discerning fact from fiction.

Conspiracy Theories Have Entered Mainstream Conversation Because of the Internet   66
David Greene
Although still largely fringe, some conspiracy theories that spread online can become widely enough believed to enter mainstream debate and thinking.

In Order to Fight Holocaust Denial, It Is Important to Understand How It Spreads   70
Joe Mulhall
The internet and the rise of far-right nationalism have given new life to Holocaust denial. In order to counter it, society must meet it where it is spreading.

No: Conspiracy Theories Had Traction Long Before the Internet

Conspiracy Theories Have Always Spread Via Mass Communication, Including Print Publishing   73
Matt Novak
The widely known conspiracy theory that the moon landing was faked is an example of how conspiracy theories spread before the internet simply through the efforts of those who believe them.

The Internet Doesn't Spread Conspiracy Theories, It Just Provides a Forum for Those Who Believe Them   78
Karen Douglas
The internet allows like-minded groups to communicate, including those who believe in conspiracy theories. This does not mean the internet is the cause of conspiracy theories.

The Root Paranoia of Conspiracy Theories Has Long Been a Part of American Culture   81
Brandon Sanchez

The place of conspiracy theories in the American psyche is much more complex than simple posts on the internet. The paranoia that encourages belief in conspiracy theories is an essential and longstanding aspect of American culture.

Chapter 3: Should Holocaust Denial Be Legal?

Overview: Holocaust Denial Is at Odds with History, Fact, and Tolerance   86
Scott Miller

Defined as the rejection of the fact that the Holocaust occurred, Holocaust denial is associated with hate groups, racism, and anti-Semitism. This viewpoint examines some of the ways in which Holocaust denial occurs.

Yes: Holocaust Denial and Other Forms of Speech Are Protected by the First Amendment

Laws Are Not an Effective Means of Addressing Holocaust Denial   98
Timothy Garton Ash

Though well intentioned, laws that try to bar Holocaust denial are not effective and do harm to free expression.

Laws Banning Holocaust Denial Are at Odds with the Constitution and Free Speech   102
Kenneth Lasson

As explained in this excerpted viewpoint, the language and spirit of the First Amendment as widely interpreted does not allow for censorship, such as the banning of Holocaust denial.

Using Laws to Shape Historical Memory Can Have Sinister Consequences   110
Eric Heinze

Using "memory laws" to dictate how citizens can remember and discuss a country's historical events—including the Holocaust—threatens democratic values. Citizens should have the right to challenge accepted historical narratives.

No: Holocaust Denial Is an Inherently Harmful Ideology That Encourages Hate and Intolerance

Those Who Deny the Holocaust Are Denying History and in Some Countries Face Legal Consequences 113

Volker Wagener

Punishments vary across countries that outlaw Holocaust denial, but the root crime is the same in each instance.

Holocaust Denial Is Not Just Speech—It Poses a Threat to Society 117

Jeremy Bilfield

Although sometimes framed as being simply a matter of free speech, Holocaust denial is associated with domestic terrorist groups and hate groups and as such must be taken seriously as a threat.

Holocaust Denial Is Hate Speech That Should Not Be Defended 125

Elana Heideman

While Facebook has been relatively tolerant toward Holocaust denial on the platform, the author and those interviewed in this viewpoint indicate that this is at odds with Facebook's claim that hate speech will not be tolerated.

The Limits of Free Speech in the Classroom and Beyond 132

Jennifer Rich

This viewpoint examines the case of a New Jersey public school teacher who was fired for encouraging Holocaust denial among his students. As this case shows, the right to free speech has limitations.

Chapter 4: Can Conspiracy Theories Be Stopped?

Overview: Many Factors Are at Play in Conspiracy Theorizing 137

Kendra Cherry

Belief in conspiracy theories is more common than you might expect and often linked to feelings of powerlessness or alienation.

Yes: There Are Ways to Refute Conspiracy Theories

It Is Difficult, but Possible, to Counter Conspiracy Theories in Court 144

Enrique Armijo

With a high burden of proof that might make it hard for some to find resolution, the courts are a difficult but possible way for some to counter conspiracy theories spread about them, such as the victims of gun violence.

Education Could Be a Path to Reducing Widespread Belief in Conspiracy Theories — 148

Tania Lombrozo

Studies have found links between higher levels of education and lower belief in conspiracy theories.

No: Conspiracy Theories Are Rooted in Beliefs Rather than Reason and Consequently Can't Be Effectively Stopped

Fighting the Irrational Can Be Difficult — 152

Phil Whitby

Conspiracy theories are born in part out of a belief that one is more rational than others, which can make countering these theories difficult.

Inequality Plays a Role in the Spread of Conspiracy Theories — 156

University of Cambridge

Studies have found links between low levels of equality and high levels of belief in conspiracy theories, suggesting that factors contributing to the spread of these beliefs are more complex than simply changing one person's mind.

Trusting in Intuition Encourages Belief in Conspiracy Theories — 160

R. Kelly Garrett

According to a recent study, most Americans base their beliefs on their intuition rather than evidence. This trust in intuition combined with political beliefs makes individuals particularly susceptible to believing conspiracy theories.

Organizations to Contact — 164
Bibliography — 168
Index — 171

Foreword

"Controversy" is a word that has an undeniably unpleasant connotation. It carries a definite negative charge. Controversy can spoil family gatherings, spread a chill around classroom and campus discussion, inflame public discourse, open raw civic wounds, and lead to the ouster of public officials. We often feel that controversy is almost akin to bad manners, a rude and shocking eruption of that which must not be spoken or thought of in polite, tightly guarded society. To avoid controversy, to quell controversy, is often seen as a public good, a victory for etiquette, perhaps even a moral or ethical imperative.

Yet the studious, deliberate avoidance of controversy is also a whitewashing, a denial, a death threat to democracy. It is a false sterilizing and sanitizing and superficial ordering of the messy, ragged, chaotic, at times ugly processes by which a healthy democracy identifies and confronts challenges, engages in passionate debate about appropriate approaches and solutions, and arrives at something like a consensus and a broadly accepted and supported way forward. Controversy is the megaphone, the speaker's corner, the public square through which the citizenry finds and uses its voice. Controversy is the life's blood of our democracy and absolutely essential to the vibrant health of our society.

Our present age is certainly no stranger to controversy. We are consumed by fierce debates about technology, privacy, political correctness, poverty, violence, crime and policing, guns, immigration, civil and human rights, terrorism, militarism, environmental protection, and gender and racial equality. Loudly competing voices are raised every day, shouting opposing opinions, putting forth competing agendas, and summoning starkly different visions of a utopian or dystopian future. Often these voices attempt to shout the others down; there is precious little listening and considering among the cacophonous din. Yet listening and considering, too, are essential to the health of a democracy. If controversy is democracy's lusty lifeblood, respectful listening and careful thought are its higher faculties, its brain, its conscience.

Current Controversies does not shy away from or attempt to hush the loudly competing voices. It seeks to provide readers with as wide and representative as possible a range of articulate voices on any given controversy of the day, separates each one out to allow it to be heard clearly and fairly, and encourages careful listening to each of these well-crafted, thoughtfully expressed opinions, supplied by some of today's leading academics, thinkers, analysts, politicians, policy makers, economists, activists, change agents, and advocates. Only after listening to a wide range of opinions on an issue, evaluating the strengths and weaknesses of each argument, assessing how well the facts and available evidence mesh with the stated opinions and conclusions, and thoughtfully and critically examining one's own beliefs and conscience can the reader begin to arrive at his or her own conclusions and articulate his or her own stance on the spotlighted controversy.

This process is facilitated and supported in each Current Controversies volume by an introduction and chapter overviews that provide readers with the essential context they need to begin engaging with the spotlighted controversies, with the debates surrounding them, and with their own perhaps shifting or nascent opinions on them. Chapters are organized around several key questions that are answered with diverse opinions representing all points on the political spectrum. In its content, organization, and methodology, readers are encouraged to determine the authors' point of view and purpose, interrogate and analyze the various arguments and their rhetoric and structure, evaluate the arguments' strengths and weaknesses, test their claims against available facts and evidence, judge the validity of the reasoning, and bring into clearer, sharper focus the reader's own beliefs and conclusions and how they may differ from or align with those in the collection or those of classmates.

Research has shown that reading comprehension skills improve dramatically when students are provided with compelling, intriguing, and relevant "discussable" texts. The subject matter of these collections could not be more compelling, intriguing, or urgently relevant to today's students and the world they are poised to inherit. The anthologized articles also provide the basis for stimulating, lively, and passionate classroom debates. Students who are compelled to anticipate objections to their own argument and identify the flaws in those of an opponent read more carefully, think more critically, and steep themselves in relevant context, facts, and information more thoroughly. In short, using discussable text of the kind provided by every single volume in the Current Controversies series encourages close reading, facilitates reading comprehension, fosters research, strengthens critical thinking, and greatly enlivens and energizes classroom discussion and participation. The entire learning process is deepened, extended, and strengthened.

If we are to foster a knowledgeable, responsible, active, and engaged citizenry, we must provide readers with the intellectual, interpretive, and critical-thinking tools and experience necessary to make sense of the world around them and of the all-important debates and arguments that inform it. We must encourage them not to run away from or attempt to quell controversy but to embrace it in a responsible, conscientious, and thoughtful way, to sharpen and strengthen their own informed opinions by listening to and critically analyzing those of others. This series encourages respectful engagement with and analysis of current controversies and competing opinions and fosters a resulting increase in the strength and rigor of one's own opinions and stances. As such, it helps readers assume their rightful place in the public square and provides them with the skills necessary to uphold their awesome responsibility—guaranteeing the continued and future health of a vital, vibrant, and free democracy.

Introduction

> *"I'm not a conspiracy theorist—I'm a conspiracy analyst."*
>
> -Gore Vidal, American writer and intellectual

Children are taught from a young age that it is important to tell the truth. But as we age, we realize that the truth isn't always so clear; sometimes those in power aren't fully honest, or a piece of conventional wisdom is later revealed as being untrue. Reality is often messy and complicated, sometimes defying logic and challenging how we see our world.

This sense that the truth isn't always what it seems is the basis of conspiracy theories, or non-mainstream beliefs about history, politics, or another key facet of society. Conspiracy theories can include mildly offbeat beliefs—such as the idea that Area 51 is used to house alien life forms—or those more sinister, such as the belief in a secret group of people who run the world known as the Illuminati. Some become famous enough to be part of our collective conscious and pop culture, including the "true" identity of those who assassinated President John F. Kennedy or the idea that the moon landing was faked. Others remain on the fringes of society due to their incendiary nature, such as the myth that vaccines cause autism. There are even conspiracy theories that verge on hate speech. An example of a conspiracy theory that many consider dangerous is Holocaust denial, or the theory that the Holocaust carried out by Nazi Germany did not occur.

Conspiracy theories are not new. In fact, they have been around for centuries; there is evidence that what we would now

Introduction

call conspiracy theories spread within Ancient Rome.[1] But today, conspiracy theories can spread rapidly via the internet, and some websites have emerged as key places where theorists communicate. Some, such as 4chan, have been linked to violence and extremism. Whereas in the past conspiracy theorists may pick up a magazine or book and perhaps meet with a few people to discuss a theory, today believers are able to immerse themselves fully in an online community that agrees with and reinforces their ideas. This echo chamber effect has led to conspiracy theories spreading wider and quicker. They have also found greater traction as drivers of public debate.

Conspiracy theories—including Holocaust denial—challenge our ideas about honesty, belief, and free speech. Experts debate whether conspiracy theories pose a threat to public health and safety, and how best to address the challenge posed by beliefs held by a small but often passionate minority. Although most beliefs themselves do not pose a threat, someone who believes a particular theory could take action based on what they believe to be true. For example, anti-vaccine conspiracy theories have led to a rise in previously rare diseases like measles, and gunmen have attempted to or carried out shootings as a result of conspiracy theories about marginalized communities.

Far from being the fringe beliefs of a small minority, today we know that conspiracy theories can have a severe and sometimes deadly effect on our communities. Understanding conspiracy theories—where they come from, how they spread, who believes them, and how they might influence behavior—is critical today, as the internet makes it easier than ever for these beliefs to take root. But it is also important to understand the legal framework in which conspiracy theories exist, why it is so hard to stop these theories from spreading, and how they impact society at large.

In *Current Controversies: Holocaust Deniers and Conspiracy Theorists*, readers will find viewpoints about conspiracy theories in many forms, as well as the history of these beliefs. Readers will explore the nature of free speech, how other countries address the

15 |

issue of Holocaust denial, and the science behind who believes in conspiracies. Ultimately, the collection poses the question of what makes a conspiracy theory a threat rather than a harmless idea and how society can address this growing concern.

Notes

1. Jan-Willem van Prooijen and Karen M. Douglas, "Conspiracy theories as part of history: The role of societal crisis situations," *SAGE Memory Studies*, June 29, 2017, https://journals.sagepub.com/doi/full/10.1177/1750698017701615.

Chapter 1

Are Conspiracy Theories Dangerous?

Conspiracy Theories Have Long Been Part of American Public Discourse

Liberty Vittert

Liberty Vittert is a statistician and political commentator. She is a visiting scholar at Harvard University and a professor of the practice of data science at Washington University in St. Louis, as well as a faculty scholar at the Institute for Public Health.

Have the internet and social media created a climate where Americans believe anything is possible? With headlines citing now as the age of conspiracy, is it really true?

In a word, no.

While it may be true that the internet has allowed people who believe in conspiracies to communicate more, it has not increased the number of Americans who believe in conspiracies, according to the data available.

Current Beliefs

A "conspiracy theory" is a theory that explains an event or set of circumstances as the result of a secret plot, usually by powerful conspirators.

For example, take Pizzagate, the theory that Washington elite engaged in child sex trafficking at the basement of a D.C. pizzeria, which 9% of the American population believe to be true.

Over 29% of the American population believe there is a "Deep State" working against President Donald Trump. Nineteen percent believe that the government is using chemicals to control the population.

These conspiracy theories are not simply restricted to a fringe population. At least 50% of Americans believe in at least one

---

"Are Conspiracy Theories on the Rise in the US?" by Liberty Vittert, The Conservation, September 18, 2019, https://theconversation.com/are-conspiracy-theories-on-the-rise-in-the-us-121968. Licensed under CC BY-ND 4.0 International.

conspiracy theory, ranging from the idea that the 9/11 attacks were fake to the belief that former President Barack Obama was not born in the U.S.

Historical Data

There are no major comprehensive, longitudinal studies on Americans' attitudes toward conspiracy theories, mostly because it was not rigorously measured until about 10 to 20 years ago.

However, researchers have done a considerate amount of work in recent years in an attempt to understand this apparent phenomenon.

Political scientists Joseph E. Uscinski and Joseph M. Parent reviewed over 120 years of letters to the editor, from 1890 to 2010, for both The New York Times and the Chicago Tribune.

In over 100,000 letters, this review showed absolutely no change in the amount of conspiracy theory belief over time. In fact, the percent of letters about conspiracy theories actually declined from the late 1800s to the 1960s and has remained steady since then.

While these researchers looked at data only up until 2010, current polling has not shown any uptick in conspiracy theory belief since then.

The End Is Near?

As Uscinski and Parent pointed out, this isn't the first time Americans may have felt surrounded by conspiracies.

In 2004, the Boston Globe stated that we are in the "golden age of conspiracy theory."

In 1994, the Washington Post declared it's the "dawn of a new age of conspiracy theory."

In 1964, The New York Times said conspiracy theories had "grown weed like in this country."

The list could go on and on, but the gist is clear.

Whether it is the invention of the printing press, mass publishing, the telegraph, radio, cable, the internet or social media, researchers and the general public have historically proclaimed that this—or this, or this—new advance is the change-maker in political realities.

While the internet has certainly made discussion between conspiracy theorists easier, there is no evidence at this time that belief in these theories has increased.

Law Enforcement Indicates That Conspiracy Theories Can Be Directly Linked to Extremism

Jason Wilson

Jason Wilson is a journalist based in Oregon who has written for the Guardian.

The FBI has identified prominent conspiracy theories, including the sprawling rightwing hoax known as QAnon, as motivators for "domestic extremists" to carry out violence in the US.

The warning comes from an agency bulletin produced by the FBI's Phoenix field office, first reported by Yahoo News. It states that "anti-government, identity based, and fringe political conspiracy theories very likely motivate some domestic extremists, wholly or in part, to engage in criminal or violent activity."

The bulletin warns that "certain conspiracy theory narratives tacitly support or legitimize violent action," and that "some, but not all individuals or domestic extremists who hold such beliefs will act on them."

It further warns that conspiracy theories will continue to spread and incite violence unless social media companies make "significant efforts" to "remove, regulate, or counter potentially harmful conspiratorial content."

Examples given in the report include the October 2018 Tree of Life synagogue massacre, which the FBI describes as being motivated by the "Zionist Occupation Government conspiracy theory"; the "Pizzagate"-inspired attack on Washington's Comet Ping Pong restaurant in December 2016; and an incident in June 2018, when a believer in the "QAnon" conspiracy theory blocked traffic at Hoover Dam in Nevada with an armored truck.

In the latter case, the bulletin says that the man "sent letters from jail containing a distinctive QAnon slogan to President Trump."

"Conspiracy theories like QAnon could fuel "extremist" violence, FBI says," by Jason Wilson, Guardian News and Media Limited, August 1, 2019. Reprinted by permission.

Elsewhere the report discusses false 2018 claims by a border militia, Veterans on Patrol, that they had discovered a child sex trafficking camp near Tucson, Arizona, and the 2012 mass shooting at Sandy Hook Elementary in Connecticut, following which "conspiracy theorists who believed the shooting was a government hoax harassed and threatened family members of the slain victims."

Currently, several families of Sandy Hook victims are suing the conspiracy-minded broadcaster Alex Jones for what they say is his role in promoting "false flag" narratives—baseless claims that the shooting was covert operation aimed at deceiving and disarming Americans.

The bulletin accords social media a central role in promoting conspiracy theories to a wider audience. It states: "The advent of the Internet and social media has enabled promoters of conspiracy theories to produce and share greater volumes of material via online platforms that larger audiences of consumers can quickly and easily access."

As a result, the bulletin says, "it is logical to assume that more extremist-minded individuals will be exposed to potentially harmful conspiracy theories, accept ones that are favorable to their views, and possibly carry out criminal or violent actions."

The QAnon conspiracy theory, which has emerged in the Trump era, is based on posts by an anonymous user on the 4chan and 8chan websites that believers attempt to decipher. While the QAnon narrative is sprawling and incoherent, many believers hold that Donald Trump is leading a behind-the-scenes fight against elements of the "deep state," including figures such as Hillary Clinton and the former FBI director James Comey.

Recently, Trump has acted in ways that have encouraged believers to think that he is sympathetic to their cause. At a Greenville rally on 17 July, Trump singled out a "beautiful baby" whose jumpsuit was adorned with the "Q" symbol. And earlier this week, Trump retweeted an account that promoted QAnon.

FBI critics, though, worry that the bulletin exhibits the same excesses as previous reports identifying threats from so-called "black identity extremists" and other groups.

Michael German is a former FBI officer and a fellow at the Brennan Center for Justice. He called the bulletin "troubling," saying that "it continues to promote the concept of radicalization—that it's bad ideas that put people on the path to violence."

From the perspective of law enforcement officers, German said, "all it does is ramp up the fear of people whose ideas are strange."

He also said the logic of the bulletin promoted a baseless fear of the internet and further justified mass surveillance: "If the spread of ideas is the problem, then preventing the spread of ideas is the solution.

"Are there conspiracy theorists who commit violence? Yes. But you're talking about a small amount of cases alongside millions of people who believe in conspiracy theories," German added, saying that such reports "seem to have the function of getting the FBI over the one hurdle the Justice Department has imposed" in protecting first amendment activity.

The FBI bulletin concludes with the bleak prediction that "conspiracy theories very likely will emerge, spread, and evolve in the modern information marketplace over the near term, fostering anti-government sentiment, promoting racial and religious prejudice, increasing political tensions, and occasionally driving both groups and individuals to commit criminal or violent acts."

It does hold out hope that "significant efforts by major social media companies and websites to remove, regulate, or counter potentially harmful conspiratorial content" might change this assessment.

Reports Indicate a Connection Between Conspiracy Theories and Domestic Terrorism

Luke Barnes

Luke Barnes is a journalist who covers politics and the political far right.

For the first time, an FBI intelligence bulletin has assessed that fringe, internet-based conspiracy theories pose a domestic terror threat that "[encourage] the targeting of specific people, places and organizations, thereby increasing the risk of extremist violence against such targets."

The intelligence bulletin was written by the FBI's Phoenix Field Office and released in May, but was first reported by Yahoo News on Thursday. It specifically mentions Pizzagate, the conspiracy that the Clintons and other elite Democrats were indulging in child sacrifice at a D.C. pizzeria, as well as a host of other terms common on fringe, far-right internet ecosystems like False Flags, Zionist Occupied Government, and, of course, QAnon.

For those lucky enough to not spend their days following the latest QAnon news, a brief primer: QAnon is the theory that President Donald Trump, along with Attorney General William Barr, the U.S. military, and a shadowy insider known only as "Q," are all secretly working to take down a Deep State cabal, made up primarily of Democrats, who are controlling the world and also like to traffic and/or eat children.

Supposed promises by "Q," posted first on fringe sites like 4chan and 8chan, keep failing to come to fruition, but that has done little to dampen the popularity of the conspiracy, both online and off. QAnon supporters make frequent appearances at Trump rallies, and the president keeps adding fuel to the fire by

"FBI warns that conspiracy theories like QAnon pose a domestic terror threat," by Luke Barnes, ThinkProgress, August 1, 2019. Reprinted by permission.

re-tweeting QAnon accounts on Twitter and thereby—at least in the eyes of Q adherents—validating the theory.

While it's easy to laugh at, QAnon and other fringe conspiracies have motivated some very real-world violence.

As the FBI memo notes, in December 2016, a man entered Comet Ping Pong in Washington, DC—the restaurant supposedly at the center of Pizzagate—with an AR-15 rifle, firing a shot and pointing his rifle at an employee. The man was later arrested and pleaded guilty to federal weapons charges in March 2017.

In June 2018, a QAnon supporter in an armored truck blocked the Hoover Dam Bypass, armed with several firearms and magazines of ammunition. After a 90-minute standoff with police, he fled to Arizona where he was arrested. He has since been charged with terrorism as well as aggravated assault, unlawful flight, and weapons offenses.

As ThinkProgress reported last year, a QAnon-affiliated group also harassed police officers and civic leaders in Arizona over claims that the Deep State was operating a child sex camp in the desert there. A QAnon believer is also believed to have used the conspiracy as inspiration to gun down alleged New York crime boss Francesco Cali in March.

Travis View, a QAnon researcher who also co-hosts the QAnon Anonymous podcast, said he was relieved by the memo, as it showed that the Feds understood the real dangers that QAnon poses.

"It was an unknown beforehand whether the FBI or law enforcement was taking QAnon and other conspiracy-driven extremist movements seriously at all," View told ThinkProgress. "This is the first confirmation that the feds are very aware of QAnon and the threat they pose."

View described QAnon as "very much like a decentralized cult."

"They get separated from their families and get taken down this rabbit hole to super delusional beliefs that cause them to do violence and violent things ... most QAnon followers are harmless, they're just shacked up in their room, but a few of them get so delusional that they act out in the real world."

The FBI's memo also specifically mentions how the internet has allowed these theories to thrive.

"The advent of the Internet and social media has enabled promoters of conspiracy theories to produce and share greater volumes of material via online platforms that larger audiences of consumers can quickly and easily access," the report reads. "Based on the increase volumed and reach … it is logical to assume that more extremist-minded individuals will be exposed to potentially harmful conspiracy theories, accept ones that are favorable to their views, and possibly carry out criminal or violent actions as a result."

To be clear, QAnon is not a movement that explicitly encourages members to engage in acts of violence; a large percentage of Q-related content simply encourages followers to "enjoy the show" that is always just about to begin.

However, as proven by recent mass attacks in New Zealand, Pittsburgh, and California—to name just a few—it only takes one self-radicalized individual to carry out a major terror attack, especially at a time of heightened political polarization, a point that both View and the FBI made.

"Because some conspiracy theories are highly partisan in nature, political developments, including those surrounding major election cycles such as the 2020 presidential election, likely will impact the direction of these conspiracy theories and the potential activities of extremists who subscribe to them," the report reads.

"My most important takeaway [from the memo] is that this isn't a fading threat," View said. "It is a growing threat. As the political season and rhetoric gets more heated, conspiracy theories get an over-sized importance in people's lives—it's certainly something to watch out for."

The FBI assessment concludes it is "very likely" that, in the future, domestic extremists will be motivated, whether wholly or in part, by "anti-government, identity based and fringe political conspiracy theories."

And as for QAnon? Despite its continual failure to deliver on its promises, View predicts it won't be going anywhere any time soon. The FBI assessment, he noted, was already being explained away by QAnon followers as more evidence of the Deep State, or something planted as a way to move the media to ask Trump about Q, a long-held ambition of QAnon followers.

"The 'Clinton body-count' conspiracy theory, [which claims multiple people close to the Clintons have died under 'mysterious circumstances,' suggesting the Clintons have something to do with it], was created in early 1990s and it trended last week on Twitter, so these sort of conspiracy theories, when they catch on and resonate with a community, they don't go away," View said.

He added, "I have no idea when they might give up the game, but if I were to speculate based on psychological research [into conspiracy theories and followers], this is something with us for at least a generation."

Conspiracy Theories Change How Some People Behave in Dangerous Ways

Timothy Callaghan and Matt Motta

Timothy Callaghan is an assistant professor of public health at Texas A&M University. Matt Motta is an assistant professor of political science at Oklahoma State University.

Over 1,160 cases of measles have been confirmed in the U.S. in 2019. That is more measles cases in just seven months than any full year this decade, and, more problematically, more than all U.S. measles cases from 2010-2013 and 2015-2017 combined.

Lawmakers in some states, such as Washington and New York, are already stepping in to combat the outbreak by eliminating certain exemptions from vaccination. We will soon know whether these new policies produce higher vaccination rates.

However, a fundamental question remains: Why are some parents—despite the scientific community's conclusions that childhood vaccines are safe—putting their children at risk by not vaccinating them in the first place? Public health experts and health behavior scholars like us have been trying to solve this mystery for years.

Why Don't Some Parents Vaccinate?

Religious beliefs or barriers to accessing health services certainly explain the actions of some, but these factors do not explain the behavior of most parents who choose not to vaccinate. Instead, recent academic research suggests that most parents who display vaccine hesitancy—by either refusing to vaccinate their children or delaying vaccination past recommended vaccine

---

"Conspiracy theories and fear of needles contribute to vaccine hesitancy for many parents," by Timothy Callaghan and Matt Motta, The Conversation, August 1, 2019. https://theconversation.com/conspiracy-theories-and-fear-of-needles-contribute-to-vaccine-hesitancy-for-many-parents-120864. Licensed under CC BY-ND 4.0 International.

schedules—do so because of misinformation about vaccine safety, their political ideology, the influence of social media, and other factors like economic circumstances and trust.

As important as these factors are, we wondered if the behavior of vaccine-hesitant parents might also have deeper, psychological origins. For that reason, in a new paper published in Social Science and Medicine, we analyzed the possibility that parental decisions to delay vaccinating children could be driven by three underlying psychological factors: conspiratorial thinking, needle sensitivity and moral purity.

Facts Don't Matter When People Don't Trust Them

People with conspiratorial styles of thinking tend to believe that the government, businesses and other powerful actors conspire to influence a wide range of social and political events in the world around us. They don't necessarily believe any one particular conspiracy theory—such as the belief that NASA faked the Moon landing, or that someone other than Lee Harvey Oswald killed President John F. Kennedy. Still, because many conspiracy theories involve collusion between powerful actors, these people are more likely than the typical American to believe in conspiracy theories generally.

Given the variety of conspiracy theories surrounding vaccine safety, including disproven theories that vaccines cause autism or that pharmaceutical companies are hiding the dangers of vaccines, we wanted to test whether parents with tendencies toward conspiratorial styles of thought may be more likely to delay vaccinating their children because they have internalized these conspiracies.

Needle Fear and Vaccine Behavior

In addition, we also wanted to see whether parents who are afraid of or are otherwise averse to needles themselves—what psychologists call "needle sensitivity"—are less likely to vaccinate their children when they are supposed to. Prior research suggests that as many as 24% of adults have a fear of needles and that up to 90% of 15-18 month old children and 45% of children aged 4 to 6 are seriously distressed by injections.

Given these statistics, we wanted to see whether some parental decisions not to vaccinate weren't necessarily because they thought vaccines were dangerous, but because the parents were afraid of needles and didn't want to put their children through something that causes them so much distress.

The Role of Bodily Sanctity

Finally, we wanted to test whether a notion called moral purity—an aversion to actions that violate bodily sanctity—might also explain parental anti-vax behavior.

Individuals with high levels of moral purity try to avoid experiences that induce disgust, violate sanctity or corrupt the body. While vaccines are widely regarded as safe, we, like some other scholars studying related topics, hypothesized that some might see the injection of the disease antigens found in vaccines as a violation of the body's purity that should be avoided in their children.

Psychological Predictors of Parental Vaccine Behavior

To test our hypotheses, we asked more than 4,000 American parents in a September 2018 survey about the vaccination decisions they made for their children and why they made those decisions. Specifically, we asked parents if they had ever delayed vaccinating their children, if they had only vaccinated their children because they had to for school, if they had chosen their child's doctor based on their willingness to delay vaccinating, and if they would be willing to relocate their families so their child could attend a school that does not require vaccination.

Before asking these questions, we also gave survey respondents a series of questions designed to measure conspiratorial thinking, needle sensitivity and moral purity, as well as standard demographic questions.

In support of our expectations, we found that parents with high levels of conspiratorial thinking were 15% more likely to report delaying their children's vaccinations. They were also 11% more likely to report having chosen their doctors based on their willingness to delay, 25% more likely to report only vaccinating their children so they can enroll in school, and 18% more likely to claim that they would be willing to relocate to a new school district.

We also found that parents' psychological dispositions toward needles influenced reported anti-vaccination behavior. Parents in our study with high levels of sensitivity toward needles were between 14-16% more likely to engage in the each of the delay behaviors included in our study. This would suggest that if needle-free vaccine delivery mechanisms were more widespread, we might get many of these children their vaccines on time. Inconsistent with our predictions, we found no evidence that parents' beliefs in moral purity altered their vaccine decision-making for their children, broadly speaking.

A Difficult Process

Our research suggests that anti-vaccine attitudes have deeply grounded psychological origins, which may be quite difficult to change. Consequently, our work identifies an important challenge for medical professionals, health departments and scientists: How can they convince vaccine hesitant parents to vaccinate their children, when it is unlikely that they'll be able to make parents stop fearing needles, or to stop endorsing a conspiratorial way of thinking?

One possibility is to present information about vaccines to parents strategically, using the psychological factors identified here as important determinants of anti-vaccine behavior as a guide. For example, if we know that parents who are prone to thinking in conspiratorial ways are less likely to want to vaccinate their children, efforts to encourage childhood vaccination may be more successful if we avoid making mention of scientific studies, which parents might see as motivated by ulterior motives, or tying information to health departments (which these parents might find untrustworthy).

Figuring out which communication strategies are most effective for different audiences is something academics and science communicators still need to test. We hope, however, that our work offers a useful starting point for doing precisely this.

Conspiracy Theories Spread Quickly, Sow Doubt, and Dehumanize the Victims of Tragedies

The Information Disorder Lab Team

The Information Disorder Lab (ID Lab) is part of the Shorenstein Center at Harvard University's John F. Kennedy School of Government. It aims to identify, track, and analyze the spread of disinformation on the internet.

It would be ludicrous if it wasn't so malicious: Fringe websites and social media users dismissed the migrant families who got caught up in skirmishes at the U.S.-Mexican border as "paid crisis actors" taking part in a staged hoax.

That phrase is a dog-whistle reference to the 2012 mass shooting at Sandy Hook Elementary School, where conspiracy mongers derisively described child victims as crisis actors who faked a deadly incident to score political points. The "crisis actor" term has circulated on social media after other high-profile violence in recent years, including the Marjory Stoneman Douglas High School and Pulse Night Club shootings in Florida, and the Boston Marathon bombing. The goal appears to be to sow doubt about basic facts with "false flag" allegations as well as to harass and intimidate opponents and victims—and to fire up allies in the process.

From the Mexican border at San Diego, a Reuters photo of a woman fleeing spewing tear gas canisters on Sunday became fodder for a meme pointing out purportedly suspicious anomalies in the background, including journalists wearing gas masks, as evidence of the "hoax." (Journalists routinely wear protective gear in such potential confrontations.)

"Digital Border Battles," by the ID Lab Team, Shorenstein Center on Media, Politics and Public Policy, Harvard Kennedy School, November 30, 2018. https://shorensteincenter.org/digital-border-battles/. Licensed under CC BY-ND 3.0. © 2020 The Shorenstein Center.

Twitter user @bahamamills said, "What we are seeing are simply paid crisis actors and the left are falling for it like BREAKING NEWS on @CNN." That was retweeted more than 400 times. The claim gained traction even though journalists were on the ground alongside the migrants on Sunday, witnessing and capturing the tense border showdown in photos and video. The far-right news site The Gateway Pundit's headline declared: "Hoaxed: The 'Illegal Alien Mom with Barefoot Kids' Photo was a Setup—Another Staged #FakeNews Production" (22.1K Facebook shares).

The hoax narrative spread fast. An article on the right-wing Daily Wire news site asking whether the confrontation was staged circulated on Facebook. The article cited tweets speculating about details in the photo.

The rapid spread of these stories involved multiple social media platforms. Tweets discussing the claim numbered in the thousands, with some of them receiving hundreds or thousands of retweets each. YouTube commentators created video reports such as one from Lisa Haven, who has a news channel with more than 376K subscribers. Her video is titled: "LIES Everywhere: Migrants Slam the Border, Fake Pictures, Fake Narratives…Bombshell!" The video received more than 81K views and gained 1.3K comments by Friday morning.

Other bare-bones videos dissected the purportedly staged photo, including Martin Brodel (2.6K views), ramzpaul (10.4K views), and An0maly—News Analysis & Hip-hop (41.1K views). Conservative pages on Facebook also released videos that racked up large view counts. This Daily Caller video got 589K views and this video shared by Comedian Bryan Dey got 226K views. Several video commentators complained that mainstream news coverage left out the fact that some migrants threw rocks and other projectiles at U.S. border agents, prompting the tear gas. Many of these videos have comment streams that serve as enraged echo chambers for viewers.

Chatter on alternative social media platforms has also been busy, although this is more difficult to quantify. A 4chan

Are Conspiracy Theories Dangerous?

thread received over 170 replies, and a Reddit post received more than 40 upvotes. Conversation has also occurred on Discord.

Within 48 hours, a meme competition was launched to portray the running family in ways that demonize illegal immigration. The account has since been suspended. Prior to the suspension, nasty images poured in—including one from the parody Twitter account of a non-existent Georgia congressman @RepStevenSmith, dropping the migrant family into a Ku Klux Klan image.

Beyond the crisis actor claim, there were other examples of mis- and disinformation that swirled across social media in the midst of the border clash:

- Twitter users complained that some migrants in Sunday's melee had chanted "Si se puede," Spanish for "Yes, it can be done," and claimed that to be an order from former President Barack Obama, whose campaign slogan was "Yes we can." In fact, "Si se puede" dates back at least to Cesar Chavez's farmworker movement in the 1960s and '70s, and has long been a frequent chant at demonstrations across Latin America.
- Some sought to underscore the story line that an "invasion" was looming: A "newsflash" on the far-right site Natural News said 90 percent of the migrant caravan members amassed at the border were "military-aged males." (The U.S. Department of Homeland Security says about half of those in the caravan are single men, who include 270 with "criminal histories, including known gang membership.") A meme claimed that President Trump had temporarily closed the entire border; while the president did threaten to close the complete border, in fact authorities only closed the San Ysidro border in San Diego for a few hours.
- A Twitter user with 37.9K followers posted about a U.S. Border Patrol agent being killed by rock throwers, as if it were part of the current unrest. That incident actually occurred on the Texas border in 2017. Some comments chided the user for the misleading post. Other Twitter users posted a

photo of a border agent injured by a thrown rock without noting it was from an incident in 2013.
- For its part, the anti-Trump left also fell into some angry hyperbole: Some complained that U.S. border agents had used a powerful tear gas to attack defenseless migrants. In fact, anti-riot tear gas was used numerous times on the border during the Obama administration without an outcry.

Conspiracy theories alleging hoaxes and false flag tactics are certainly not new. Such claims echoed after the 9-11 terror attacks in the United States. But the huge difference is the role social media and fragmented, polarized websites have played over the last decade in hyping the suspicions of and radicalizing participants.

Conspiratorial allegations have come from the left, too. After the shooting of five police officers in Dallas in 2016 by a man who declared himself angry over blacks being shot by police, some speculated on Twitter about a possible false flag operation, saying without evidence that the government may have been behind the shootings to undermine the Black Lives Matter movement.

The crisis actor claim leveled against the migrants was nurtured by two months of increasing social media agitation and demeaning memes targeting the members of the caravan, from its emergence in Honduras. These conversations contributed to a narrative of impending invasion, complete with a red-starred tank, being met by right-wing citizen militias deploying to the U.S.-Mexico border to support U.S. soldiers sent by President Trump. Some social media users exaggerated the size of the caravan (alleging it to be 40,000 strong), and the threat it posed (gang members).

The crisis actor accusation often serves to dehumanize victims and deflate the gravity of real-world tragedies. In that sense, it echoes the memes and other forms of disinformation that the Information Disorder Lab has encountered since its launch.

People with Certain Psychological Traits Are Likely to Believe in Conspiracy Theories

Joshua Hart

Joshua Hart is an assistant professor of psychology at Union College in Schenectady, New York.

Here's a theory: President Barack Obama was not born in the United States. Here's another: Climate change is a hoax. Here's one more: The "deep state" spied on Donald Trump's campaign, and is now trying to destroy his presidency.

Who believes this stuff? Conspiracy theories have been cooked up for ages, but for the first time in history, we have a president who has regularly endorsed them. Assuming that President Donald Trump's preoccupation is genuine, he shares it with many fellow Americans. What explains it?

I'm a psychologist who studies, among other things, people's worldviews and belief systems. I wanted to figure out why some people gobble up conspiratorial explanations, while others dismiss them as the raving of lunatics.

Consistency In Views

By and large, people gravitate toward conspiracy theories that seem to affirm or validate their political views. Republicans are vastly more likely than Democrats to believe the Obama "birther" theory or that climate change is a hoax. Democrats are more likely to believe that Trump's campaign "colluded" with the Russians.

But some people are habitual conspiracists who entertain a variety of generic conspiracy theories.

For example, they believe that world politics are controlled by a cabal instead of governments, or that scientists systematically

"Something's going on here: Building a comprehensive profile of conspiracy thinkers," by Joshua Hart, The Conversation, September 24, 2018. https://theconversation.com/somethings-going-on-here-building-a-comprehensive-profile-of-conspiracy-thinkers-101287. Licensed under CC BY-ND 4.0 International.

deceive the public. This indicates that personality or other individual differences might be at play.

In fact, some people seem to be downright devoted to conspiracy theories. When conspiracy maven Alex Jones' content was recently banned from several social media websites, the popularity of his Infowars news app skyrocketed.

Scientific research examining the nature of the "conspiratorial disposition" is abundant, but scattershot. So in a pair of new studies, and with help from my student Molly Graether, I tried to build on previous research to piece together a more comprehensive profile of the typical conspiracy theory believer, and for that matter, the typical non-believer.

Common Traits

We asked more than 1,200 American adults to provide extensive information about themselves and whether they agreed with generic conspiratorial statements. We tried to measure as many personal factors as possible that had been previously linked to conspiracy belief. Looking at many traits simultaneously would allow us to determine, all else being equal, which ones were most important.

Consistent with previous research, we found that one major predictor of conspiracy belief was "schizotypy." That's a constellation of traits that include a tendency to be relatively untrusting, ideologically eccentric and prone to having unusual perceptual experiences (e.g., sensing stimuli that are not actually present). The trait borrows its name from schizophrenia, but it does not imply a clinical diagnosis.

Schizotypy is the strongest predictor of conspiracy belief. In addition to experiencing the world in unusual ways, we found that people higher in schizotypy have an elevated need to feel unique, which has previously been linked with conspiracism. Why? Probably because believing in non-mainstream ideas allows people to stand out from their peers, but at the same time take refuge in a community of like-minded believers.

In our studies, conspiracy believers were also disproportionately concerned that the world is a dangerous place. For example, they were more likely to agree that "all the signs" are pointing to imminent chaos.

Finally, conspiracists had distinct cognitive tendencies: They were more likely than nonbelievers to judge nonsensical statements as profound—for example, "wholeness quiets infinite phenomena"—a tendency cheekily known as "bullshit receptivity."

They were also more likely to say that nonhuman objects—triangle shapes moving around on a computer screen—were acting intentionally, as though they were capable of having thoughts and goals they were trying to accomplish.

In other words, they inferred meaning and motive where others did not.

Is Trump a Conspiracy Thinker?

Although we can't know how he would score on our questionnaires, President Trump's public statements and behavior suggest that he fits the profile fairly well.

First, he does display some schizotypal characteristics. He is famously untrusting of others. Donald Trump Jr. has described how his father used to admonish him in kindergarten not to trust anyone under any circumstances. The elder Trump is also relatively eccentric. He is a unique politician who doesn't hew consistently to party lines or political norms. He has espoused unusual ideas, including the theory that people have a limited lifetime reservoir of energy that physical exercise depletes.

President Trump also seems to see the world as a dangerous place. His campaign speeches warned about murderous rapist immigrants flooding across the border and black communities being in "the worst shape" they've ever been. His inauguration address described a hellish landscape of "American carnage."

Holocaust Deniers and Conspiracy Theorists

Chaos Needs Comfort

The dismal nature of most conspiracy theories presents a puzzle to psychologists who study beliefs, because most belief systems—think religion—are fundamentally optimistic and uplifting. Psychologists have found that people tend to adopt such beliefs in part because they fulfill emotional goals, such as the need to feel good about oneself and the world. Conspiracy theories don't seem to fit this mold.

Then again, if you are a person who looks at the world and sees chaos and malevolence, perhaps there is comfort in the notion that there is someone to blame. If "there's something going on," then there is something that could be done about it.

Perhaps, then, even the darkest and most bizarre conspiracy theories offer a glint of hope for some people.

Take the "QAnon" theory that has recently received a flurry of media attention. This theory features a nightmare of pedophile rings and satanic cults. But some adherents have adopted a version of the theory that President Trump has it all under control.

If our research advances the understanding of why some people are more attracted to conspiracy theories than others, it is important to note that it says nothing about whether or not conspiracy theories are true.

After the Watergate scandal brought down a president for participating in a criminal conspiracy, the American public learned that seemingly outlandish speculation about the machinations of powerful actors is sometimes right on the money.

And when a conspiracy is real, people with a conspiracist mindset may be among the first to pick up on it—while others get duped. The rub is that the rest of the time, they might be duping themselves.

Conspiracy Theories Are Not Harmful by Nature and Can Even Hold Those in Power Accountable

Daniel Cohnitz

Daniel Cohnitz is a professor of theoretical philosophy at Utrecht University in the Netherlands.

The NSA spies on you. Before Edward Snowden leaked classified information in 2013, which confirmed this claim, many would probably have shrugged it off as a "mere" *conspiracy theory*. What about now? Is the theory that the NSA spies on you *still* a conspiracy theory, now that it is a widely held (and apparently well-evidenced) belief?

It seems common to think that it's not. That Caesar was murdered by a conspiracy of Roman senators, or that 9/11 was the outcome of a conspiracy among members of al-Quaeda does not make these historical accounts *conspiracy theories*. For many, the latter requires that there is an element of speculation, perhaps paranoia in the belief of such theory.

Interestingly, most philosophers who work on conspiracy theories disagree with that common understanding of the term. They find it hard to identify features that make conspiracy theories an intrinsically bad explanation type, in part because some initially suspicious conspiracy theories (like, perhaps, the theory that the NSA is spying on you) later turned out to be true. Instead, these philosophers argue that "conspiracy theory" should be defined widely: *a conspiracy theory is the explanation of an event that cites conspiring agents as a salient cause*. Consequently, we are all conspiracy theorists. Everyone who believes that some historical event came about thanks to the successful secret collaboration of

---

"Are Conspiracy Theories a Force for the Good?" by Daniel Cohnitz, The Philosophers' Magazine 80:52-57 (2018). Reprinted by permission.

several individuals believes in a conspiracy theory and thus is a conspiracy theorist, and surely everyone believes this of some event.

Since some of these accounts are true and known to be true (e.g. that the assassination of Caesar was due to a conspiracy), believing in a conspiracy theory as such can't be irrational or misguided. *In principle* then there is nothing wrong with conspiracy theories or belief in such theories. Of course, sometimes conspiracy theories are mistaken and sometimes they are believed on the basis of insufficient evidence, but that is the possible fate of every theory. There is nothing that makes conspiracy theories particularly irrational, doubtful or fishy, just because they are conspiracy theories.

Accordingly, attempts by psychologists and sociologists to investigate the psychological and social profile of conspiracy believers might be seen as nothing but a witch-hunt. In a recent public statement, a group of social epistemologists and sociologists (Matthew R. X. Dentith, Lee Basham, David Coady, Ginna Husting, Martin Orr, Kurtis Hagen, Marius Raab), even argue that such witch-hunt endangers our (development towards an) open society. In their paper, *Social Science's Conspiracy-Theory Panic: Now They Want to Cure Everyone*, which was published last year by the *Social Epistemology Review & Reply Collective*, they say:

> [W]e believe that it is not conspiracy theorizing that is the danger, but rather the pathologizing response to conspiracy theories.
>
> The antidote to whatever problems conspiracy theories present is vigilance, not some faux intellectual sophistication which dismisses conspiracy theories out of hand. It's really quite simple when you think about it: conspiracy theorising is essential to the functioning of any democracy, or indeed any ethically responsible society.

The argument behind it is that conspiracy theorising keeps the public in critical control of the people in power and might prevent the latter from doing serious harm. Such critically minded citizens should be interested in developing an even more open society with institutions that exercise mutual control, one might add, because that's what makes conspiring much harder. So, is conspiracy theorising not actually a danger to our current political system, but rather a force for the good?

I believe that these philosophers and sociologists are right in thinking that the problem with (certain) conspiracy theories is not their *explanation type*, and that the fault of conspiracy theories needs to be identified on a case by case basis in the many ways in which people make mistakes when theorising. But from that it doesn't follow that conspiracy theorising in a society is largely a force for the good or that we should welcome it in the interest of an open society.

On the contrary, *conspiracy theorising is a danger to the institutions of the open society*, and this can be shown on the basis of social epistemological considerations alone.

In any case, it can already be made plausible on the basis of empirical evidence. Have a look around at countries that were on a path to open, democratic societies with separation of power, freedom of speech, etc. and in which conspiracy theories have played a significant role in political campaigns that led to political change. The examples I have in mind are Turkey, Hungary, Poland, and the USA. In all these cases, the political change induced was then not at all towards a general strengthening of the institutions of open societies so that these could better exercise mutual control. On the contrary, the change was towards a mutilation of these institutions and a development away from an open society towards a closed society that displays elements of an autocracy.

Now, obviously, in all these cases there is a variety of factors that came together and led to the particular political development. I don't want to argue that it is only due to conspiracy theorising that these countries got off the path to an open society. But I do want to argue that conspiracy theorising has been a causal factor in this process. There is an epistemological explanation for the turn these societies took.

To see this, reflect for a minute on the things you know and why you know them. Most of that knowledge stems from testimony.

A lot of it stems from the testimony of people that you do not know personally but that you have trusted anyway because you realized that they have the relevant expertise on the matter. You get knowledge from reading the news, watching TV, reading books, attending classes in college or school, talking to a physician or a lawyer. The fact that you attain *knowledge* on the basis of what you read, see, and hear there is due to the fact that the people that certain institutions (like the media, the universities, colleges, and schools) present as experts actually are experts.

Now, unless we have intimate insight into these institutions ourselves and know how journalists, scientists, lawyers, physicians, etc. work; how they are trained and selected and what track record they have of getting things right, we are typically not in a position to evaluate ourselves whether trust in these experts is justified. But then how do we realize their expertise? Well, typically we do that on testimony as well. You picked it up from people that you already trusted on a personal level—like your parents and others in your close vicinity—who told you that you can *also* trust these institutions and their experts. Your parents, or those others in your close vicinity had themselves then either direct personal reasons to trust specific experts (perhaps based on personal acquaintance) or also indirect reasons for such trust, based on the testimony of yet others.

For such networks of trust to lead to *knowledge*, this must somewhere bottom out in (collective) direct knowledge of the reliability of the procedures used to generate the knowledge in the first place. But, typically, most people do not have that direct knowledge.

You learn from your physician that you should vaccinate your children because the benefits far outweigh the possible health risks this might pose for your children. You don't know what the evidence for that claim is, you don't typically check the data that your physician bases her recommendations on. And that makes sense: if presented with the empirical data and their statistical analysis, most people would be unable to see whether the data seems uncorrupted and whether the conclusions drawn from it are justified. They are better off believing their physician, because *she is the expert*.

In *her* judgment, to be sure, your physician will be relying on other expert testimony herself. The statistical methods she is using were developed and checked by statisticians who themselves used mathematical methods that *they* did not verify, etc. This division of cognitive labour in our complex societies is not just a matter of saving us valuable time. It is a matter of necessity. We cannot check all the interdependent knowledge claims in our society because it would be *impossible* to acquire all the expertise that we'd need for doing this.

So, on the one hand, our society with its division of cognitive labour and its institutions that train and systematically educate highly specialized and knowledgeable experts, and that provide incentive structures and selection processes which lead to reliable and trustworthy performance of these experts, generates a lot of knowledge. However, on the other hand, this does not by itself guarantee that everyone can automatically benefit from the generated knowledge. One needs to happen to stand in a number of stable enough personal trust relations of the right kind in order to be able to get oneself to trust in the output of these knowledge generating institutions.

After all, for all that most people directly know about academia, the media and the schools, and for all knowledge of facts they observed themselves and that they can use in order to verify claims made by members of these institutions, this "generated knowledge" could all just be a major scam. Which brings us back to our conspiracy theorists.

In many of the contemporary problematic conspiracy theories, the relevant conspirators are many, if not all of the institutions that, in open societies, are supposed to exercise mutual control. Big pharma lobbies politicians and pays scientists and the media to convince everyone else that vaccinations are beneficial and pretty harmless to the recipient in order to make profit.

If you think you have reason to believe such a conspiracy theory, this has repercussions for your epistemic situation. Let us assume that you falsely believe that vaccination is harmful for the recipient but that this is covered up in the way and for the reasons described above.

The heuristic rules that the relevant institutions provide for the identification of expertise (e.g. having a scientific degree, being employed at such an institution, etc.) will then become useless to you (unless, of course, you'd see that the institutions react appropriately to the alleged fraud by firing corrupt scientists or journalists, which, of course, they don't, since your theory is false). It will also impact the way you view the rest of the trust network. Those members of your family or your immediate vicinity who initially provided a pathway to benefit from the knowledge produced by the institutions of your society are now unreliable. You don't need to think that they tried to mislead you, it is sufficient to think that they too have been misled. And indeed, if pressed on details of your new vaccination conspiracy theory they don't have direct evidence that they can provide against it, right? So, they naively believed on hearsay, and you can now "enlighten" them.

As a result, however, you are cut off the knowledge generated in your society. Presumably you have a residual core of personal trust relations left. At least those relations with your fellow "truthers", the people who put you initially in the know about the purported large-scale conspiracy that is going on in your society. Your interest will be that none of the institutions that have failed you will get in between you and those you personally trust. It will be rational for you to prefer an information flow architecture that gives you unfiltered and immediate access to information, coming from persons to which you (believe to) stand in a direct trust relation.

This is rational for someone who believes a false conspiracy theory, because for her it seems that the institutions that are meant to filter, mediate, or cross-check information, are all corrupt or broken. Note that even though personal trust is necessary to participate in the knowledge generated in your society, your trust in its institutions is not *completely* based on testimony. For one thing, you may have direct evidence that the experts in your society can't be completely incompetent. Technology typically works and makes progress, occasionally things turn out the way that politicians promised such that you experience the consequences of that improvement yourself. But normally you also observe that when things go wrong, there are correcting mechanisms: journalists report, say, that scientists falsified their data, and politics and academia react properly. Studies are retracted, perhaps laws are changed in order to ensure higher standards, policies that were based on the misinformation are changed, the scientists get punished or fired. Thus, in order to have trust in the institutions of your society, you don't need to believe that everything is always going well. But you need to believe that *when* things go wrong, the mutual control mechanisms of these institutions will detect and correct the mistakes, and you have occasionally evidence that this indeed happens.

Now, as we already noted before, in case that you believe a *false* conspiracy theory, none of this happens. The vaccination program doesn't stop, scientists just deny the allegations, politicians even discuss to introduce a formal duty to vaccinate in order to force vaccination sceptics like you to comply. You can directly observe that the system is broken. Why should you want corrupt institutions to become even stronger?

If you get someone who you personally trust into power—perhaps even into presidency—you will not be interested in having that person's actions controlled by corrupt institutions. The influence of these institutions would need to be reduced, their political power limited, the swamp must be drained. It will be rational to prefer the destruction of (what actually are) institutions of the open society. That is precisely what we can empirically observe when open societies take an autocratic turn based on false conspiracy theories.

We started with the observation that conspiracies sometimes happen and that, therefore, belief in a conspiracy theory can't be irrational just because you believe that certain events are orchestrated by a conspiracy. Indeed, uncovering actual conspiracies in our society is important. Conspiracy theorising might occasionally be onto something, and when it is we need to know. So, shouldn't one conclude that conspiracy theorising is an important force for the good in our society? Shouldn't we tolerate the growth of false conspiracy theories as a harmless (and sometimes even somewhat entertaining) side-effect of an important control mechanism?

I have argued that this would be naïve. False conspiracy theories are dangerous for the institutions of open societies. They undermine and eventually destroy the trust network that is necessary for these institutions to perform their primary functions. As a consequence, their very existence may be put in question. It is thus necessary that we understand why (some) people are prone to believe false conspiracy theories even though the evidential situations for these theories seems objectively bad. This will require epistemological, sociological and psychological research on conspiracy theories and their believers. This is not a witch hunt.

Conspiracy Theorists Can See Reason

Mark Lorch

Mark Lorch is a professor of science communications and chemistry at the University of Hull in England.

I'm sitting on a train when a group of football fans streams on. Fresh from the game—their team has clearly won—they occupy the empty seats around me. One picks up a discarded newspaper and chuckles derisively as she reads about the latest "alternative facts" peddled by Donald Trump. The others soon chip in with their thoughts on the US president's fondness for conspiracy theories. The chatter quickly turns to other conspiracies and I enjoy eavesdropping while the group brutally mock flat Earthers, chemtrails memes and Gwyneth Paltrow's latest idea.

Then there's a lull in the conversation, and someone takes it as an opportunity to pipe in with: "That stuff might be nonsense, but don't try and tell me you can trust everything the mainstream feeds us! Take the moon landings, they were obviously faked and not even very well. I read this blog the other day that pointed out there aren't even stars in any of the pictures!"

To my amazement the group joins in with other "evidence" supporting the moon landing hoax: inconsistent shadows in photographs, a fluttering flag when there's no atmosphere on the moon, how Neil Armstrong was filmed walking on to the surface when no-one was there to hold the camera.

A minute ago they seemed like rational people capable of assessing evidence and coming to a logical conclusion. But now things are taking a turn down crackpot alley. So I take a deep breath and decide to chip in.

"Actually all that can be explained quite easily … "

"Why people believe in conspiracy theories – and how to change their minds," by Mark Lorch, The Conversation, August 18, 2017. https://theconversation.com/why-people-believe-in-conspiracy-theories-and-how-to-change-their-minds-82514. Licensed under CC BY-ND 4.0 International.

They turn to me aghast that a stranger would dare to butt into their conversation. I continue undeterred, hitting them with a barrage of facts and rational explanations.

"The flag didn't flutter in the wind, it just moved as Buzz Aldrin planted it! Photos were taken during lunar daytime— and obviously you can't see the stars during the day. The weird shadows are because of the very wide-angle lenses they used which distort the photos. And nobody took the footage of Neil descending the ladder. There was a camera mounted on the outside of the lunar module which filmed him making his giant leap. If that isn't enough then the final clinching proof comes from the Lunar Reconnaissance Orbiter's photos of the landing sites where you can clearly see the tracks that the astronauts made as they wandered around the surface.

"Nailed it!" I think to myself.

But it appears my listeners are far from convinced. They turn on me, producing more and more ridiculous claims. Stanley Kubrick filmed the lot, key personnel have died in mysterious ways, and so on …

The train pulls up in a station, it isn't my stop but I take the opportunity to make an exit anyway. As I sheepishly mind the gap I wonder why my facts failed so badly to change their minds.

The simple answer is that facts and rational arguments really aren't very good at altering people's beliefs. That's because our rational brains are fitted with not-so-evolved evolutionary hard wiring. One of the reasons why conspiracy theories spring up with such regularity is due to our desire to impose structure on the world and incredible ability to recognise patterns. Indeed, a recent study showed a correlation between an individual's need for structure and tendency to believe in a conspiracy theory.

Take this sequence for example:

0 0 1 1 0 0 1 0 0 1 0 0 1 1

Can you see a pattern? Quite possibly—and you aren't alone. A quick twitter poll (replicating a much more rigourous study)

Are Conspiracy Theories Dangerous?

suggested that 56% of people agree with you—even though the sequence was generated by me flipping a coin.

It seems our need for structure and our pattern recognition skill can be rather overactive, causing a tendency to spot patterns—like constellations, clouds that looks like dogs and vaccines causing autism where in fact there are none.

The ability to see patterns was probably a useful survival trait for our ancestors—better to mistakenly spot signs of a predator than to overlook a real big hungry cat. But plonk the same tendency in our information rich world and we see nonexistent links between cause and effect—conspiracy theories—all over the place.

Peer Pressure

Another reason we are so keen to believe in conspiracy theories is that we are social animals and our status in that society is much more important (from an evolutionary standpoint) than being right. Consequently we constantly compare our actions and beliefs to those of our peers, and then alter them to fit in. This means that if our social group believes something, we are more likely to follow the herd.

This effect of social influence on behaviour was nicely demonstrated back in 1961 by the street corner experiment, conducted by the US social psychologist Stanley Milgram (better known for his work on obedience to authority figures) and colleagues. The experiment was simple (and fun) enough for you to replicate. Just pick a busy street corner and stare at the sky for 60 seconds.

Most likely very few folks will stop and check what you are looking at—in this situation Milgram found that about 4% of the passersby joined in. Now get some friends to join you with your lofty observations. As the group grows, more and more strangers will stop and stare aloft. By the time the group has grown to 15 sky gazers, about 40% of the by-passers will have stopped and craned their necks along with you. You have almost certainly seen the same effect in action at markets where you find yourself drawn to the stand with the crowd around it.

The principle applies just as powerfully to ideas. If more people believe a piece of information, then we are more likely to accept it as true. And so if, via our social group, we are overly exposed to a particular idea then it becomes embedded in our world view. In short social proof is a much more effective persuasion technique than purely evidence-based proof, which is of course why this sort of proof is so popular in advertising ("80% of mums agree").

Social proof is just one of a host of logical fallacies that also cause us to overlook evidence. A related issue is the ever-present confirmation bias, that tendency for folks to seek out and believe the data that supports their views while discounting the stuff that doesn't. We all suffer from this. Just think back to the last time you heard a debate on the radio or television. How convincing did you find the argument that ran counter to your view compared to the one that agreed with it?

The chances are that, whatever the rationality of either side, you largely dismissed the opposition arguments while applauding those who agreed with you. Confirmation bias also manifests as a tendency to select information from sources that already agree with our views (which probably comes from the social group that we relate too). Hence your political beliefs probably dictate your preferred news outlets.

Of course there is a belief system that recognises logical fallacies such as confirmation bias and tries to iron them out. Science, through repetition of observations, turns anecdote into data, reduces confirmation bias and accepts that theories can be updated in the face of evidence. That means that it is open to correcting its core texts. Nevertheless, confirmation bias plagues us all. Star physicist Richard Feynman famously described an example of it that cropped up in one of the most rigorous areas of sciences, particle physics.

> Millikan measured the charge on an electron by an experiment with falling oil drops and got an answer which we now know not

Are Conspiracy Theories Dangerous?

to be quite right. It's a little bit off, because he had the incorrect value for the viscosity of air. It's interesting to look at the history of measurements of the charge of the electron, after Millikan. If you plot them as a function of time, you find that one is a little bigger than Millikan's, and the next one's a little bit bigger than that, and the next one's a little bit bigger than that, until finally they settle down to a number which is higher.

Why didn't they discover that the new number was higher right away? It's a thing that scientists are ashamed of—this history—because it's apparent that people did things like this: When they got a number that was too high above Millikan's, they thought something must be wrong and they would look for and find a reason why something might be wrong. When they got a number closer to Millikan's value they didn't look so hard.

Myth-Busting Mishaps

You might be tempted to take a lead from popular media by tackling misconceptions and conspiracy theories via the myth-busting approach. Naming the myth alongside the reality seems like a good way to compare the fact and falsehoods side by side so that the truth will emerge. But once again this turns out to be a bad approach, it appears to elicit something that has come to be known as the backfire effect, whereby the myth ends up becoming more memorable than the fact.

One of the most striking examples of this was seen in a study evaluating a "Myths and Facts" flyer about flu vaccines. Immediately after reading the flyer, participants accurately remembered the facts as facts and the myths as myths. But just 30 minutes later this had been completely turned on its head, with the myths being much more likely to be remembered as "facts."

The thinking is that merely mentioning the myths actually helps to reinforce them. And then as time passes you forget the context in which you heard the myth—in this case during a debunking—and are left with just the memory of the myth itself.

To make matters worse, presenting corrective information to a group with firmly held beliefs can actually strengthen their view, despite the new information undermining it. New evidence creates inconsistencies in our beliefs and an associated emotional discomfort. But instead of modifying our belief we tend to invoke self-justification and even stronger dislike of opposing theories, which can make us more entrenched in our views. This has become known as the as the "boomerang effect"—and it is a huge problem when trying to nudge people towards better behaviours.

For example, studies have shown that public information messages aimed at reducing smoking, alcohol and drug consumption all had the reverse effect.

Make Friends

So if you can't rely on the facts how do you get people to bin their conspiracy theories or other irrational ideas?

Scientific literacy will probably help in the long run. By this I don't mean a familiarity with scientific facts, figures and techniques. Instead what is needed is literacy in the scientific method, such as analytical thinking. And indeed studies show that dismissing conspiracy theories is associated with more analytic thinking. Most people will never do science, but we do come across it and use it on a daily basis and so citizens need the skills to critically assess scientific claims.

Of course, altering a nation's curriculum isn't going to help with my argument on the train. For a more immediate approach, it's important to realise that being part of a tribe helps enormously. Before starting to preach the message, find some common ground.

Meanwhile, to avoid the backfire effect, ignore the myths. Don't even mention or acknowledge them. Just make the key points: vaccines are safe and reduce the chances of getting flu by between 50% and 60%, full stop. Don't mention the misconceptions, as they tend to be better remembered.

Also, don't get the opponents gander up by challenging their worldview. Instead offer explanations that chime with their preexisting beliefs. For example, conservative climate-change

Are Conspiracy Theories Dangerous?

deniers are much more likely to shift their views if they are also presented with the pro-environment business opportunities.

One more suggestion. Use stories to make your point. People engage with narratives much more strongly than with argumentative or descriptive dialogues. Stories link cause and effect making the conclusions that you want to present seem almost inevitable.

All of this is not to say that the facts and a scientific consensus aren't important. They are critically so. But an awareness of the flaws in our thinking allows you to present your point in a far more convincing fashion.

It is vital that we challenge dogma, but instead of linking unconnected dots and coming up with a conspiracy theory we need to demand the evidence from decision makers. Ask for the data that might support a belief and hunt for the information that tests it. Part of that process means recognising our own biased instincts, limitations and logical fallacies.

So how might my conversation on the train have gone if I'd heeded my own advice… Let's go back to that moment when I observed that things were taking a turn down crackpot alley. This time, I take a deep breath and chip in with.

"Hey, great result at the game. Pity I couldn't get a ticket."

Soon we're deep in conversation as we discuss the team's chances this season. After a few minutes' chatter I turn to the lunar landing conspiracy theorist "Hey, I was just thinking about that thing you said about the moon landings. Wasn't the sun visible in some of the photos?"

He nods.

"Which means it was daytime on the moon, so just like here on Earth would you expect to see any stars?"

"Huh, I guess so, hadn't thought of that. Maybe that blog didn't have it all right."

CHAPTER 2

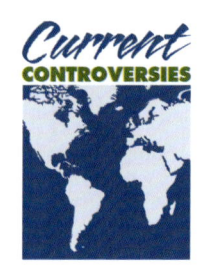

Does the Internet Spread Conspiracy Theories?

The Internet Interacts with Conspiracy Theories in Unique Ways

Joe Uscinski

Joe Uscinski is an American political scientist and an associate professor of political science at the University of Miami. His research focuses on conspiracy theories and includes the book American Conspiracy Theories.

We're often told we're living in a post-truth world where conspiracy theories have replaced facts, expertise, and rationality. This may or may not be true, but there is no strong evidence showing that people today reject facts in favor of conspiracy theories more than they have in past historical eras.

The assertion that we are living in the age of conspiracy theory is often taken as an article of faith. To support the idea that conspiracy theories have hit an apex, the ability of the internet to effortlessly spread misinformation far and wide is often trotted out as exhibit A.

Since the unlikely election of Donald Trump to the presidency, many blamed the spread of online conspiracy theories and fake news for Hillary Clinton's unexpected loss. Their basic argument is that because voters were exposed to incorrect information, they made choices they otherwise would not have made in the voting booth. If those voters had the right information, they would have made better choices (and presumably not for Trump).

Some evidence suggests voters were exposed to a great deal of conspiracy theories and fake news in 2016, but it is not clear what effect—if any—exposure to these falsehoods had on their political decision making. Nonetheless, social media companies have been pressured by Congress to police the information on their

"Is the Internet Driving a New Age of Conspiracy Theory?" by Joe Uscinski, ARC Digital Media Inc., February 11, 2019. Reprinted by permission.

sites, often in ways that severely limit the free transference of ideas. The public has been all too willing to cede this power to legislators. As could have been predicted whenever government threatens information purveyors, much of the speech that has been banned is critical of government. But if the internet has not had the negative effects on people that its critics claim, then government intervention is unwarranted (I would say that it probably wouldn't be warranted anyway, but that is another matter).

It is unquestionably true that the internet has given us the ability to communicate unfiltered ideas instantaneously to the far reaches of the planet. But what do we really know about the role of the internet in changing people's beliefs? Is the internet making conspiracy theories more popular than before? Has the internet turned people into conspiracy-mongers? The simple answer to these questions is *probably not*, and here are three reasons why.

There Is No Evidence That Beliefs of a Conspiratorial Kind—i.e., Conspiracy Beliefs— Have Increased Since the Dawn of the Internet Age

As I argue in my book *American Conspiracy Theories*—co-written with Joseph M. Parent—it is not clear that beliefs in conspiracy theories are increasing. While one conspiracy theory is not representative of the whole, consider for example belief in Kennedy assassination theories. Immediately following the assassination of President Kennedy, polls showed that belief in a conspiracy to kill the president was a majority belief; in the decades that followed as many as 80 percent of Americans believed there was a conspiracy rather than a lone gunman. None of this required the internet.

If the internet increases conspiratorial thinking, we would have expected the internet age to bring with it an uptick in people believing JFK assassination conspiracy theories or at least to have maintained belief around 80 percent. But since the roll-out of the internet in the 1990s, belief in JFK assassination conspiracy theories has declined about 20 points. Yes, the assassination has become more distant in our collective past, but there continues to be no shortage of talk about Kennedy conspiracy theories on the internet or in more traditional media to keep it alive. Belief is down regardless.

Kennedy assassination theories are just one small slice of the conspiracy theory pie, but conspiracy beliefs writ large don't show much evidence of having gone up as the internet made its way into everyone's home. The level of belief in conspiracy theories is an empirical issue, and such levels could conceivably rise and fall over time. Perhaps in a few years their levels will markedly rise or precipitously fall, but until we have evidence of such dynamics we should not assume conspiracy beliefs are higher or lower now than at any other time.

The Internet Has Authoritative Information Too

One might get the impression from much journalism that the internet is populated exclusively by conspiracy theories, fake news, and dubious information. It isn't. The internet allows for unprecedented access to the best and most authoritative information humans have from doctors, lawyers, governments, and scientists. Prior to the advent of the internet, it was much more tempting to rely on village wisdom because experts were hard to come by. That's just not the case anymore, and we need to thank the internet for that.

However, it's true that the internet comes with a lot of content dedicated to conspiracy theories and other forms of dubious information. Dubious information is always a problem and we should not gloss over its impact. But just because a conspiracy theory is available on the internet doesn't mean anyone is looking at it. For example, the *New York Times* website is currently ranked about 33rd in the U.S. and 118th globally for web traffic; Alex Jones' *InfoWars* site, perhaps the most popular conspiracy theory dedicated website is ranked a distant 942 in the U.S. and 3,454th worldwide.

Social media allows people to develop and share their own conspiracy theories too, but the effect of this should not be overrated either. One can go onto social media any time of day and find new conspiracy theories brewing, but most of those theories will fail to make it to dawn of the next day. As much as Twitter and Facebook allow new conspiracy theories to be openly shared; they are great at squashing conspiracy theories as well. Consider for example the theory that Barack Obama killed Justice Antonin Scalia in 2016. That theory attracted attention for a short while, but quickly became sterile. Part of the issue is that sharing conspiracy theories on social media can generate new believers, but it can also lead to immediate ridicule and rebuttal. Some scholars suspect that the internet may be better at killing conspiracy theories than it is at propagating them.

Ideologies Still Matter

The internet allows people to invent their own information environments; they pick their friends, who they follow, what websites they access. People's ideologies tend to drive these choices so that people immerse themselves into online environments that favor what they already believe. Even when they do come into contact with unwanted conspiracy theories, it is not clear that these theories have the sweeping effects that critics claim because people's ideologies are good at rejecting discordant ideas anyway.

This is not to say that dubious ideas are harmless or have no effects. People who absorb inaccurate information will sometimes believe it, and worse, act on it. Once dubious ideas are lodged in a person's head, they can be difficult to dislodge. But these effects are much more nuanced than they are often made out to be.

The internet has been widely used in the U.S. for more than 20 years. If the impact was what some accounts say it is, we would have fallen off of the conspiracy theory cliff years ago (we haven't). No doubt the internet has changed society in many ways, but it is unwarranted to blame the internet for every perceived social ill. To put this in perspective, the invention of paper, the printing press, telephone, radio, and television all led contemporary critics to claim that each of these was to blame for a breakdown of public opinion and/or morals. The truth is that more and better communication has been accompanied by social improvements along numerous dimensions. We should all fight dubious ideas when we see them, but at the same time we should not blame old problems on new technologies.

The Internet Is Making It Possible for Falsehoods to Spread Quicker Than Ever Before

David Dunning

David Dunning is a professor of psychology at the University of Michigan.

In the hours since I first sat down to write this piece, my laptop tells me the National Basketball Association has had to deny that it threatened to cancel its 2017 All-Star Game over a new anti-LGBT law in North Carolina—a story repeated by many news sources including the Associated Press. The authenticity of that viral video of a bear chasing a female snowboarder in Japan has been called into question. And, no, Ted Cruz is not married to his third cousin. It's just one among an onslaught of half-truths and even pants-on-fire lies coming as we rev up for the 2016 American election season.

The longer I study human psychology, the more impressed I am with the rich tapestry of knowledge each of us owns. We each have a brainy weave of facts, figures, rules and stories that allows us to address an astonishing range of everyday challenges. Contemporary research celebrates just how vast, organized, interconnected and durable that knowledge base is.

That's the good news. The bad news is that our brains overdo it. Not only do they store helpful and essential information, they are also receptive to false belief and misinformation.

Just in biology alone, many people believe that spinach is a good source of iron (sorry, Popeye), that we use less than 10 percent of our brains (no, it's too energy-guzzling to allow that), and that some people suffer hypersensitivity to electromagnetic radiation (for which there is no scientific evidence).

"Why the internet isn't making us smarter—and how to fight back," by David Dunning, The Conversation, April 15, 2016, https://theconversation.com/why-the-internet-isnt-making-us-smarter-and-how-to-fight-back-56713. Licensed under CC BY-ND 4.0 International.

But here's the more concerning news. Our access to information, both good and bad, has only increased as our fingertips have gotten into the act. With computer keyboards and smartphones, we now have access to an Internet containing a vast store of information much bigger than any individual brain can carry—and that's not always a good thing.

Better Access Doesn't Mean Better Information

This access to the Internet's far reaches should permit us to be smarter and better informed. People certainly assume it. A recent Yale study showed that Internet access causes people to hold inflated, illusory impressions of just how smart and well-informed they are.

But there's a twofold problem with the Internet that compromises its limitless promise.

First, just like our brains, it is receptive to misinformation. In fact, the World Economic Forum lists "massive digital misinformation" as a main threat to society. A survey of 50 "weight loss" websites found that only three provided sound diet advice. Another of roughly 150 YouTube videos about vaccination found that only half explicitly supported the procedure.

Rumor-mongers, politicians, vested interests, a sensationalizing media and people with intellectual axes to grind all inject false information into the Internet.

So do a lot of well-intentioned but misinformed people. In fact, a study published in the January 2016 Proceedings of National Academy of Science documented just how quickly dubious conspiracy theories spread across the Internet. Specifically, the researchers compared how quickly these rumors spread across Facebook relative to stories on scientific discoveries. Both conspiracy theories and scientific news spread quickly, with the majority of diffusion via Facebook for both types of stories happening within a day.

Making matters worse, misinformation is hard to distinguish from accurate fact. It often has the exact look and feel as the truth.

In a series of studies Elanor Williams, Justin Kruger and I published in the *Journal of Personality and Social Psychology* in 2013, we asked students to solve problems in intuitive physics, logic and finance. Those who consistently relied on false facts or principles—and thus gave the exact same wrong answer to every problem—expressed just as much confidence in their conclusions as those who answered every single problem right.

For example, those who always thought a ball would continue to follow a curved path after rolling out of a bent tube (not true) were virtually as certain as people who knew the right answer (the ball follows a straight path).

Defend Yourself

So, how so we separate Internet truth from the false?

First, don't assume misinformation is obviously distinguishable from true information. Be careful. If the matter is important, perhaps you can start your search with the Internet; just don't end there. Consult and consider other sources of authority. There is a reason why your doctor suffered medical school, why your financial advisor studied to gain that license.

Second, don't do what conspiracy theorists did in the Facebook study. They readily spread stories that already fit their worldview. As such, they practiced confirmation bias, giving credence to evidence supporting what they already believed. As a consequence, the conspiracy theories they endorsed burrowed themselves into like-minded Facebook communities who rarely questioned their authenticity.

Instead, be a skeptic. Psychological research shows that groups designating one or two of its members to play devil's advocates—questioning whatever conclusion the group is leaning toward—make for better-reasoned decisions of greater quality.

If no one else is around, it pays to be your own devil's advocate. Don't just believe what the Internet has to say; question it. Practice a disconfirmation bias. If you're looking up medical information about a health problem, don't stop at the first diagnosis that looks right. Search for alternative possibilities.

Seeking Evidence to the Contrary

In addition, look for ways in which that diagnosis might be wrong. Research shows that "considering the opposite"—actively asking how a conclusion might be wrong—is a valuable exercise for reducing unwarranted faith in a conclusion.

After all, you should listen to Mark Twain, who, according to a dozen different websites, warned us, "Be careful about reading health books. You may die of a misprint."

Wise words, except a little more investigation reveals more detailed and researched sources with evidence that it wasn't Mark Twain, but German physician Markus Herz who said them. I'm not surprised; in my Internet experience, I've learned to be wary of Twain quotes (Will Rogers, too). He was a brilliant wit, but he gets much too much credit for quotable quips.

Misinformation and true information often look awfully alike. The key to an informed life may not require *gathering* information as much as it does *challenging* the ideas you already have or have recently encountered. This may be an unpleasant task, and an unending one, but it is the best way to ensure that your brainy intellectual tapestry sports only true colors.

Conspiracy Theories Have Entered Mainstream Conversation Because of the Internet

David Greene

David Greene is a journalist, author, and the host of NPR's Morning Edition.

David Greene talks to Daily Beast reporter Will Sommer, who describes how online alt-tech sites like Gab help push conspiracy theories and alt-right ideologies from the fringes into the mainstream.

DAVID GREENE, HOST: So how do fake narratives and conspiracy theories make it from the far-right corners of the Internet to mainstream conversation or even the president's Twitter feed? This question carries new urgency after the events of recent days after a gunman killed 11 people in a Pittsburgh synagogue over the weekend.

The suspect was an active user of the social media site Gab, where he posted his anti-Semitic thoughts. Gab bills itself as a free speech alternative to Facebook and Twitter and is hardly the first place on the Internet where anti-Semitism, white nationalism and other extreme ideologies spread. We spoke earlier this morning to Will Sommer, who thinks about all this a lot. He reports on fringe right-wing media for The Daily Beast. And he's actually tracked how conspiracy theories gain traction.

Hi there, Will.

WILL SOMMER: Thanks for having me.

©2018 National Public Radio, Inc. NPR report titled "How Online Conspiracy Theories Make Their Way Into The Mainstream" by David Greene was originally published on npr.org on October 30, 2018, and is used with the permission of NPR. Any unauthorized duplication is strictly prohibited.

GREENE: So what's a good example of how this works?

SOMMER: Sure. So for example, I mean, the most obvious example right now is the caravan—the so-called caravan coming out of Honduras. This is the idea that this was some big menace, you know, an invading horde is something that really sort of bubbled up on sort of the darkest edges of the right-wing Internet with a lot of sort of hoaxes behind it. And, you know, they've kind of been pushing this idea for a couple months now. And it's only really this month that it's caught on, so much so that the president is now sending troops to fight off this sort of nonexistent invasion.

GREENE: Now, I mean, of course, the president would say sending the military somewhere is a very important decision. But you are saying that you have been able to actually track this, that the idea that this caravan is a menace was on some of these fringe sites. And you could watch it work its way into the conversation in sort of mainstream politics.

SOMMER: Absolutely. People have done analyses of this that show sort of like, you know, starting on various Facebook pages, Reddit accounts, 4chan, which is a pro-Trump Internet forum, all of these places. And they kind of hit the meme enough in the message. And then just in the past week or two, it really has caught on. You know, Representative Matt Gaetz from Florida was one of the big promoters of it. And then from there, it really took off.

GREENE: Are there other examples where you've actually seen these sort of theories work their way as high as, you know, top officials and even the White House?

SOMMER: Yeah. I think some of the most fascinating stuff happens when these weird hoaxes and conspiracy theories affect actual policy. So the president claimed after the 2016 election that he had lost the popular vote because 3 million illegal votes were cast.

And you can draw a pretty direct line from that to an InfoWars article that had originally made that claim. And then that claim then goes on to inspire the president to create the presidential voter fraud commission.

GREENE: Will, who does something about this, if anyone? I mean, if these conspiracy theories are not true, if some or all or many of them are not based on fact, who reins this in? Is it the job of the press to knock these things down? Should it fall to social media platforms to regulate what's being shared there?

SOMMER: You know, I think it's an incredibly thorny issue. I mean, we've seen in the past when the press tries to fact-check things, you often end up amplifying the hoaxes and spreading them around. And you aren't really convincing the people who believe in them already. You know, at this point, I think people have kind of decided the ball is in the court of the social media companies. But you know, they've been very reluctant to step in, understandably, into adjudicating political controversies. So I think it's a very sticky issue. I think the companies, right now, are erring more on the side of banning people and stuff like that than they were in the past.

GREENE: Are we seeing this a lot more than we used to, or has this always been going on?

SOMMER: I mean, it seems like something that has really accelerated. Obviously, we've had conspiracy theories for decades and even before that. But it's really accelerated with social media. And also, I think, the Internet and social media allows people to connect and reinforce one another's beliefs in a way they couldn't really in real life.

GREENE: Will Sommer reports on fringe right-wing media for The Daily Beast, joining us this morning in our studios in Washington.

Will, we really appreciate it.

SOMMER: Hey, thanks for having me.

In Order to Fight Holocaust Denial, It Is Important to Understand How It Spreads

Joe Mulhall

Joe Mulhall is a historian and senior researcher at the organization Hope not Hate, which is an advocacy group based in the United Kingdom.

In 1945, as the news of organised mass murder and gas chambers shocked the world, the far right's dream of a fascist future was left shattered in the ruins of Berlin.

The horrors of the Holocaust became the primary roadblock to the resurrection of fascism's besmirched ideology. Many on the far right believed then, as they do now, that if fascism was ever to rise again then the truth of the Holocaust had to be destroyed.

Since Germany's military defeat in 1945, Holocaust denial has been an attempt by surviving unreconstructed Nazis and their postwar acolytes to whitewash the monstrous crimes of the Third Reich in the hope of rehabilitating the Nazi regime.

However, denial of the Holocaust has never been a monopoly of the far right. History has taught us that antisemitism arises in many forms, and this is no less true for Holocaust denial. That's why Hope Not Hate's new book also explores denial to be found in leftwing circles, in eastern Europe and from Muslims both in Muslim-majority countries and in the west as well.

Beyond considering contemporary political, religious and geographical dimensions to Holocaust denial, one of the key findings of the book is the worrying generational shift and the changing nature of far-right Holocaust denial engendered by the explosion of the internet.

Recognising the internet's potential for reaching people at an unprecedented scale, Holocaust deniers were early adopters

"Holocaust denial is changing – the fight against it must change too," by Joe Mulhall, Guardian News and Media Limited, November 21, 2018. Reprinted by permission.

of online platforms, some as early as the 1980s. And since the 2000s social media's arrival has had a profound impact, not just on the ability of the denial community to spread their ideas but more fundamentally on the idea of, and motivation for, Holocaust denial itself.

The good news is that in the past decade there has been a noticeable decline in influence of the traditional Holocaust denial movement, drawn from among a hardcore of far-right believers. The ageing scene has struggled to rejuvenate itself while many of its most prominent activists, such as David Irving, have become less and less active, or unable to fill the venues they once did, while other major figures such as the notorious French academic Robert Faurisson have died.

Even the powerhouse organisations of the denial movement no longer hold the sway they once did. The California-based Institute for Historical Review (IHR), for example, has continued to host conferences but the majority of such events in the west are small or else subsumed into other far-right gatherings, which do not exist to specifically emphasise Holocaust "revisionism."

It has become clear that the traditional far-right Holocaust denial scene, striving towards pseudo-academic respectability amid increasing old age, has (thankfully) failed to attract new members because it has not positioned or organised itself in a way that is accessible and attractive to a younger audience.

However, Holocaust denial—and antisemitism more widely—are far from being in decline. Both are very much present in the modern far right and are central to the international far-right movement known as the alt-right.

For the new generation of online far-right activists that dwell on neo-Nazi websites such as the Daily Stormer or internet image boards such as 4Chan, the pseudo-intellectualism of traditional Holocaust denial is often now eclipsed by a style of deliberately subversive Holocaust "humour." This "for the lulz" attitude is prevalent among the young, online far right. Where once deniers went to great lengths to scientifically "prove" the Holocaust didn't happen, alt-right deniers are more likely to joke about it or even celebrate it.

A 2018 article on the Daily Stormer, for example, is titled: "Germany: British Woman Investigated for Denying Kooky Fake Shower Room Hoax," typifying the casual way in which the alt-right engages with the Holocaust and antisemitism.

Similarly, recognising the changing dynamics of communicating Holocaust denial in the social media age, a thread on the website's forum called "How would you debunk the Holocaust in 140 characters or less?" was started by a user last year.

Another fundamental difference between the nature of the alt-right's denial and the denial of more traditional far-right movements is the lack of importance placed on the Holocaust. For many traditional far-right antisemites, the Holocaust represented the primary obstacle to the resurrection of their fascist creed. However, as a result of the increasing distance from the second world war and the young age of many alt-right activists, some perceive the Holocaust as ancient history.

This view is typified by a number of tweets from the American antisemitic conspiracy theorist and white nationalist Mike Peinovich (aka Mike Enoch), noted for promoting the PizzaGate conspiracy theory, published on the UK's Holocaust Memorial Day in 2018: "Here's the thing Jews. Real or fake, I don't give a f*ck about the holocaust, mmmkay. #HolocaustMemorialDay"

For many young far-right activists the Holocaust is shorn of historical significance, diminished by time and absent from their collective consciousness, as it was not for previous generations throughout the postwar period. Far-right Holocaust denial is changing and if we are to be ready to fight back against those who seek to rewrite history for their own political ends, we have to understand how they are trying to do it.

Conspiracy Theories Have Always Spread Via Mass Communication, Including Print Publishing

Matt Novak

Matt Novak is a journalist and editor at Gizmodo.

Conspiracy theories about the Moon landing have been around for years. Decades, in fact. And while it's easier than ever to spread false stories thanks to the internet, the belief that humans never landed on the Moon is way older than the web.

How did people learn about Moon landing conspiracy theories before the internet? People of the 20th century had a strange and primitive technology known as books.

The 1974 self-published book *We Never Went to the Moon* by Bill Kaysing was the first lengthy discussion on the topic committed to paper. Kaysing, who died in 2005, was a technical writer at space contractor Rocketdyne in the 1950s, which led some people to think that Kaysing knew what he was talking about when he insisted that the Moon landings were actually filmed at a production studio in Area 51. People believed Kaysing despite the fact that he would sometimes admit he knew "zero" about rockets.

Kaysing didn't have to work too hard to convince an already skeptical public that the Apollo space program and the first Moon landing on July 20, 1969 was a sham. Americans of the late 1960s and early 1970s were already living through one of the most disheartening eras of the 20th century, with everything from the Vietnam War to the corruption of Watergate leading the average person to distrust anything their government might be telling them.

The Knight newspaper company in July 1970 found that a whopping 30 percent of Americans believed the Moon landing had been faked. And a Gallup poll in 1976 found that 28 percent of

"How Moon Landing Conspiracy Theories Spread Before the Internet," by Matt Novak, Gizmodo Media Group, July 16, 2019. Reprinted by Permission.

Americans believed that the Moon landing had been staged by the U.S. government—pretty consistent findings throughout the 1970s.

Kaysing thought he had a lot of reasons to believe the U.S. government needed to fake the Moon landing. First, he insisted that it simply wasn't possible given the technology of the day. This argument was made through a lot of hand-waving and by suggesting that his firsthand knowledge from Rocketdyne gave him some special insight.

"As a witness to many rocket engine tests at the Santa Susana lab, I saw many failures, blowups and premature engine cutoffs due to incipient disaster," Kaysing wrote in his book. "Even after the relatively modest Atlas engine cluster was accepted by the Air Force for use in the Atlas ICBM, failures occurred with repeated regularity."

But his most damning evidence that the Moon landing was a hoax was perhaps the most easy to discredit. Specifically, Kaysing wrote, repeatedly, that the absence of stars in the photos taken on the Moon proved humans never went there.

"There are no stars in any of their pictures," Kaysing told a New Jersey newspaper in 1977. "If they were taken on the moon there would have been some stars in evidence." The suggestion was that this was some kind of oversight on the part of NASA and proved that it was all fake.

The reality? There are a lot of good reasons that you don't see stars in the photos from the Moon. But people here in the 21st century probably understand that today better than they could in the 1970s. Anyone who's used a smartphone to take pictures when there's a single annoying light source can get easily frustrated. Astronauts are exposed to a lot more direct sunlight in space, so if you expose the photo using an appropriate aperture for the surface of the Moon, you're not going to capture the relatively little light from stars.

If you set the camera's aperture wide to capture the stars, you'd get something like this demonstration from a great debunker of the Moon hoax people by VideoFromSpace on YouTube.

Does the Internet Spread Conspiracy Theories?

Another one of Kaysing's claims was that acclaimed director Stanley Kubrick was probably involved in faking the Moon landings. Kubrick's 1968 movie *2001: A Space Odyssey* included some of the most impressive special effects work that had been done to date and it helped create the theory that Kubrick had actually directed the footage we know today as the Apollo landings.

"While '2001' was being filmed, Kubrick and his crew consulted with nearly 70 industrial and aerospace corporations, universities, observatories, weather bureaus, laboratories and other institutions to ensure that the film would be technically accurate," Kaysing wrote. "Had this been done for ASP without the cover of '2001', much suspicion would have been directed towards those making the inquires."

What's ASP? According to Kaysing, that stands for the "Apollo Simulation Project." In fact, Kaysing even points to the ballooning budget of the film as more evidence that Kubrick was in on the moon hoax, insinuating that the director was paid by NASA to stage a cover-up.

Kaysing's book also included photos of hotels in Las Vegas—the place where Kaysing said the astronauts lived while they were supposed to be on the Moon. In fact, Kaysing suggests that the astronauts insisted on Vegas because guys like Buzz Aldrin, Neil Armstrong, Michael Collins, and their publicity "managers" wanted to live it up in style.

Hard to argue with that, right?

Another piece of "evidence" that Kaysing spends considerable time on throughout the book is the fact that the practice sessions that astronauts conducted look like a fake Moon landing. Admittedly, I made the same joke back in 2014 before I had even heard of Kaysing's book.

And the photos really do look like prep for a fake landing. But they're not. They're just training. Obviously these photos have stuck around and are used on the internet as "evidence" even today.

Ralph Rene is another Moon hoaxer who gained prominence before most American were online, having published a book

Holocaust Deniers and Conspiracy Theorists

called *MENSA Lectures*, retitled *The Last Skeptic Of Science* after Mensa reportedly sued for using the name without permission. But it was Rene's second book, published in 1994, that made him a folk hero of the Moon hoax community. Called *NASA Mooned America!*, the book, which is still available on Amazon, has many similarities to Kaysing's work in the 1970s, but includes some even more outlandish claims.

One of the most damning pieces of evidence that Rene has? The astronauts don't look sufficiently excited upon their return. Rene published a photo to show that the astronauts were actually embarrassed that they'd just lied to the American public.

Rene explained:

> Is this the look of three men who had just returned from being the first men to walk on the Moon? The Apollo 11 crew have just returned to Earth and are talking to President Nixon from quarantine. This group is definitely not a bunch of happy campers. Could they feel ashamed about something they didn't do?

I mean, what more evidence do you need?

As the decades went on, a larger percentage of Americans came to accept that we probably landed on the Moon. By 1999, just six percent of us thought that the entire thing was a hoax. Perhaps because as technology advances, things like that seem less wild. But the conspiracy theorists are still out there, obviously. And they've got a louder voice than ever, even if their numbers have dwindled.

Kaysing and Rene are no longer around, but they both live on through the waking nightmare that is our internet. Both appear in some of the most popular Moon hoax videos currently online, including one video, "The Truth Behind the Moon Landings," that has almost a million views on YouTube as of this writing.

You clearly don't need the internet for a conspiracy theory to spread. And in an age of actual conspiracies perpetrated by powerful people, it's easy to see the appeal of conspiracy theories like the Moon hoax.

But, like it or not, we probably landed on the Moon. Why? The best evidence, aside from all the movie footage, photos, and Moon rocks, might be a simple argument. Given the camera technology of the 1960s, it would've been harder to fake the Moon landing that it would've been to just go there. Seriously.

The Internet Doesn't Spread Conspiracy Theories, It Just Provides a Forum for Those Who Believe Them

Karen Douglas

Karen Douglas is a professor of social psychology at the University of Kent in the United Kingdom.

Conspiracy theories are popular and there is no doubt that the internet has fuelled them on. From the theory that 9/11 was an inside job to the idea that reptilian humanoids rule the world, conspiracy theories have found a natural home online.

But the extent to which we can actually attribute their popularity to the internet is a question that has concerned scholars for many years. And the answer is not very straightforward. While some argue that conspiracy theories flourish on the internet and social media, there is not yet any evidence that this is true. Conspiracy theories have always been with us. But today the internet fuels them in new ways and enables the deepening of conspiracy theorising in some online communities.

A Long History

Conspiracy theories feature prominently in current political contexts, but they have a long history. Antisemitic conspiracy theories concerning the supposedly evil and controlling acts of Jewish people date back to antiquity, and still exist today. There is even good evidence that conspiracy theories were common in ancient Rome. So we know that conspiracy theories flourished perfectly well without the internet.

Contrary to what you might think, there is no evidence that people are more prone to believing in conspiracy theories now

---

"The internet fuels conspiracy theories – but not in the way you might imagine," by Karen Douglas, The Conversation, June 18, 2018. https://theconversation.com/the-internet-fuels-conspiracy-theories-but-not-in-the-way-you-might-imagine-98037. Licensed under CC BY-ND 4.0 International.

than they were prior to the internet. An analysis of published letters to the editor of the New York Times showed that, between 1897 and 2010, apart from a couple of peaks during the global depression in the late 1800s, and the fear of communism during the 1950s, conspiracy theorising had not increased. People appear to have always found conspiracy theories interesting and worth entertaining.

But there is strong evidence that some people adopt conspiracy theories more than others and that belief in conspiracy theories seems particularly strong among people with unsatisfied psychological needs.

All people need to feel that they know the truth. They also need to feel safe and secure. And people need to feel good about themselves and the groups they belong to. For people who don't have these needs met, conspiracy theories become particularly appealing. It is for these people—who may be more inclined toward conspiracy theorising in the first place—that we see the greatest impact of the internet.

How The Internet Fuels Conspiracy Theories

Conspiracy theories do not bounce indiscriminately from person to person over the internet. Not everyone reads them, and they are certainly not adopted and shared by everyone. Instead, conspiracy theories tend to be shared within communities that already agree with them. For example, a person who strongly believes that 9/11 was an inside job is likely to join an internet group and communicate with others who also agree the same. A person who does not already believe in this conspiracy theory is unlikely to join such a group, or share its material.

So, rather than increasing belief in conspiracy theories generally, the internet plays a crucial role in fostering distinct and polarised online communities among conspiracy believers. Believers share their opinions and "evidence" with other believers but are less willing to share with people who are critical of conspiracy theories. So with the internet, conspiracy groups become more homogeneous and their beliefs become even stronger over time.

To illustrate this effect, one study showed that if internet users shared conspiracy-related information, they tended to ignore information that ran contrary to the conspiracy theory. In other words, they filtered out information that was not consistent with their pre-existing views. These people also tended to share the conspiracy-related information with other conspiracy believers rather than non-believers. This style of communication creates echo chambers where information is only consumed and shared if it reinforces what people already think. In closed communication such as this, beliefs in conspiracy theories can become stronger and more separated from the opinions of non-believers.

A 2015 study showed that believers in one conspiracy theory are also more likely to share completely new, unrelated, and made-up conspiracy theories. Users who believed more traditional conspiracy theories were likely to share new, clearly false and easily verifiable conspiracy theories, such as the idea that infinite energy had been discovered. The study demonstrated that conspiracy internet users are uncritically distributing and endorsing even deliberately false, extremely implausible material.

Why is this dangerous? Well, some conspiracy theories are dangerous. Consider anti-vaccine conspiracy theories proposing that vaccines are harmful and that the harms are covered up by pharmaceutical companies and governments. Even though they are false, these conspiracy theories discourage people from having their children vaccinated. Or, consider conspiracy theories that climate change is a hoax created by climate scientists to secure more research funding. Despite abundant evidence that climate change is not a hoax, these conspiracy theories discourage people from taking action to reduce their carbon footprint.

Conspiracy theories can have powerful consequences, but we are still learning about when and how people communicate conspiracy theories and why people adopt them in preference to more conventional explanations. Understanding more about how conspiracy theories move about on the internet and social networks will play a crucial part in developing the best ways to respond to them.

The Root Paranoia of Conspiracy Theories Has Long Been a Part of American Culture

Brandon Sanchez

Brandon Sanchez is a journalist with the Wall Street Journal.

The 17th-century minister Cotton Mather believed Native Americans were "conspiring with [the Devil]" to dislodge white colonists. Today, the radio host Alex Jones asserts that a coterie of state actors is drugging President Trump's Diet Cokes.

"While conspiracy theories are as old as the country itself," writes the journalist Anna Merlan in her new book *Republic of Lies*, "there is something new at work: people who peddle lies and half-truths have come to prominence, fame, and power as never before." They sit atop social-media perches and traverse the halls of 1600 Pennsylvania Avenue. Their influence wafts through the internet like a contagion through air vents. Before YouTube suspended his account last August, Jones counted 2.4 million subscribers. President Trump, a noted conspiracy theorist, commands an audience of nearly 60 million followers on Twitter (it is hard to know how many are bots).

Cataloging the president's bouts of magical thinking is like counting a stampede of antelope. Trump said former President Obama wiretapped Trump Tower in Manhattan. He said Obama was born in Kenya. He tied Ted Cruz's father to the John F. Kennedy assassination, insinuated that Bill Clinton and Joe Scarborough have killed former aides and interns, and accused Democrats of inflating the Hurricane Maria death toll. In 2017 he formed a voter fraud commission, headed by Vice President Michael R. Pence, to investigate the baseless claim that millions of people voted illegally in the 2016 election. (The commission disbanded in 2018 after finding no evidence of such fraud.)

"Review: Psst! We are all conspiracy theorists," by Brandon Sanchez, America Press Inc., March 19, 2019. Reprinted by permission.

In 2019, fabrications and phantasms are legion, hole-punching your brain until it feels like Swiss cheese. A book by QAnon, a right-wing conspiracy group, recently appeared on the Amazon bestseller list. (The book claims that Democrats run a trafficking ring and drink children's blood.) Merlan dives right into these cesspools, interviewing conspiracy theorists on cruises to Mexico, at conventions in Los Angeles and Kentucky, and across the street from the White House in Lafayette Square. She writes with such acuity that I could not stop reading: Each page pops with bizarro details and characters.

Supreme among the conspiracy theorists profiled here is the aforementioned Alex Jones, who has claimed that domestic terror attacks like the Oklahoma City bombing, the Boston Marathon bombing and the Sandy Hook massacre were government-sanctioned hoaxes, or "false flags." (In February 2019, Jones was deposed in a defamation lawsuit brought against him by the Sandy Hook families.) These denials stem from a conviction that the attacks were "part of a string of assaults on right-wing patriot groups and had been staged to justify further crackdown on those groups." Merlan writes that some conspiracists thought the suicide bombing at an Ariana Grande concert in Manchester, U.K., was a "false flag" planted by liberals to distract from the death of Democratic National Committee staffer Seth Rich.

In his seminal 1964 essay "The Paranoid Style in American Politics," the historian Richard Hofstadter wrote that "the modern right wing...feels dispossessed: America has been largely taken away from them and their kind, though they are determined to try to repossess it and to prevent the final destructive act of subversion." In *Republic of Lies*, the outlandishness of conspiratorial thinking belies the "petri dish" of an enfeebled social safety net, class immobility and racism: In Merlan's words, "the fear of losing one's place on a narrow ledge to someone seen as inferior." But paranoia is not always partisan, or even rooted in class. Merlan points to wealthy progressives like Robert De Niro and Robert F. Kennedy, Jr., who have aligned with the anti-vaccine movement.

"To go truly viral," Merlan writes, "conspiracies need a famous name or a big media outlet as an accelerant, the connective tissue that connects the fringe with the power players." When Seth Rich died, WikiLeaks agitator Julian Assange gave an interview to a Dutch TV station in which he hinted that Rich was a WikiLeaks informant. Theories proliferated online, implicating prominent Democrats like the Clintons.

Rod Wheeler, a private investigator who appeared on a D.C. Fox affiliate to discuss Rich's death, later said that "the White House had encouraged him to push the Seth Rich conspiracy theories to draw attention away from the administration's alleged Russian collusion."

Particularly distinct from the Trumpian brand of reactionary conspiracism are the suspicions minority communities harbor about their government. As a recent exhibition at the Met Breuer in New York showed, the government—often inclined toward opacity and poltroonery—has conspired against people of color, particularly African-Americans. Any account of conspiracism is incomplete without this history; Merlan devotes an illuminating chapter, called "None of it Is Crazy," to the subject.

In the 1960s and '70s, she writes, the F.B.I. targeted civil-rights leaders, at one point sending Martin Luther King, Jr., an anonymous letter urging him to commit suicide. In 2015, the agency surveilled Black Lives Matter protests using "secret spy planes." Beginning in the 1930s, the government knowingly withheld medical treatment from black men as part of a 40-year syphilis study. Under Trump, the Department of Homeland Security "gutted funding for Countering Violent Extremism, an Obama-era program that devoted resources to organizations that fight white supremacist groups."

This history of sabotage has produced its own paranoia. Merlan writes of a New Orleans community activist who testified before Congress that someone had "bombed the walls of the levee" during Hurricane Katrina. The rapper Snoop Dogg said this of flu shots: "I think they're shooting some control in you."

"A weird thing about being black," the journalist Michael Harriot tells Merlan, "is that some of it is true and some of it is not. But none of it is crazy."

To some extent, this is Merlan's point. Crazy is relative. Conspiracies do happen. The Supreme Court swung a presidential election in 2000. The George W. Bush administration invaded Iraq under false pretenses. Russia circulated political ads on Facebook in 2016. Wells Fargo employees embezzled millions of dollars from unknowing clients. So long as the powerful—and the institutions they populate—lie and hoodwink, exploit and cut corners, people will be suspicious of them.

But another question of the Trump presidency—one I've been preoccupied with—is: Do powerful people like Trump and Jones really believe the invective they're churning out? Yes? No? Probably? Are they just trying to maintain their empires and hawk merchandise? Am I a conspiracy theorist about conspiracy theorists?

Regardless, Merlan writes, these powerful peddlers are above all self-serving. In the closing lines of the book, Rush Limbaugh rails against the "climate change agenda," saying news coverage of impending Hurricane Irma is overblown, a liberal plot designed to stoke panic. A couple of days later he "evacuated Florida, steering himself out of the path of the fake storm."

CHAPTER 3

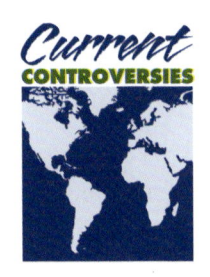

Should Holocaust Denial Be Legal?

Holocaust Denial Is at Odds with History, Fact, and Tolerance

Scott Miller

Scott Miller is an author and was a founding staff member of the United States Holocaust Memorial Museum.

Holocaust deniers claim that the Holocaust never happened-that there was no "Final Solution" or systematic plan by the Nazis to exterminate all Jews. "Hard deniers" claim that the estimated five to six million murdered Jews were actually never killed,[1] and that the Holocaust, or at least the greater part of it, is a hoax. In other versions of denial, generally referred to as "soft denials," it is contended that, while some atrocities took place, there was still no plan to annihilate the Jews. "Soft deniers" try to attribute the high death rate among Jews and others to the nature of the war itself, citing factors such as disease and starvation, which themselves are sometimes attributed to atrocities inflicted by the Allies on the Germans.

Holocaust denial is not a position based on the facts. It has no historical support. The typical denier is driven by political motivations, and in most cases espouses a right-wing, racist ideology with affinities to National Socialism. The memory of the Holocaust, which is widely regarded in the western world as the epitome of evil, is a major threat to the spread of such doctrines. Another important source of denial is the historical chain of anti-Semitism, with its recurrent inventions of conspiracy theories against the Jews, such as those contained in the Protocols of the Elders of Zion. Denial of the Holocaust, and the allegation that it is a Jewish-created "hoax," are modern versions of accusations of a Jewish conspiracy.

"Denial of the Holocaust," by Scott Miller, National Council for the Social Studies. Reprinted by permission.

For teachers, the problem of Holocaust denial can be quite complex, for several reasons. First, deniers call themselves "revisionists," which is a respectable academic term in the study of history-even though in this case, they are not revising but denying.[2] Unfortunately, their appropriation of a legitimate term has caused confusion. Moreover, deniers are denying facts, not opinions, and school curricula are not oriented toward dealing with the denial of facts. This often leaves teachers in a quandary as to how to deal with issues of denial, which can only be fully resolved by thorough knowledge of the facts of the Holocaust.

The Deniers

The key to understanding Holocaust denial is the world outlook of the deniers. Denial is inextricably linked with racist, anti-Semitic ideology. The deniers lack academic credentials for the study of the Holocaust.

The central institution of Holocaust denial in the United States is the Institute for Historical Review (IHR), located in southern California, and founded (with a deceptively scholarly name) by Willis Carto. Carto was previously a founder of the Liberty Lobby, an ultra right-wing and anti-Semitic organization. Other individuals associated with IHR and Holocaust denial are Lewis Brandon, the first director of IHR; Tom Marcellus, his successor as IHR Director; and Mark Weber, editor of the *Journal for Historical Review* (the IHR journal). Not one of the four has academic credentials relevant to the study of the Holocaust.[3]

Anti-Semitism is clearly evident in Carto's thinking. Carto once wrote: "If Satan himself had tried to create a permanent disintegration and force for the destruction of nations, he could have done no better than to create the Jews."[4] In another memo, Carto termed the Jews "public enemy No. 1."[5]

Admiration for Hitler is also widespread among IHR officials. The Liberty Lobby under Carto's influence has been described as "infiltrated by Nazis who revere the memory of Hitler."[6] In a deposition under oath in 1979, Carto acknowledged his agreement with the principles of Francis Parker Yockey, who consistently proclaimed that the Holocaust was a myth created by the Jews. In his book dedicated to Hitler, *Imperium—The Philosophy of History and Politics,* Yockey called for the establishment of an empire of Aryan nations, claiming that the Jews "live solely with the idea of revenge on the nations of the white European-American race."[7]

A number of IHR officials have been active in neo-Nazi groups. Lewis Brandon (also known as William David McCalden) was once an officer of the British neo-Nazi National Front Party. Irish-born and educated in England, Brandon has edited a number of anti-Semitic and racist publications,[8] and actively promoted the view that no Jews were gassed at Auschwitz. Mark Weber is the former editor of the *National Vanguard,* the journal of the anti-Semitic and neo-Nazi organization National Alliance.

Appeals to white racism are a common theme among these Holocaust deniers. Carto has expressed the belief that "Jews and Negroes" are at the heart of America's problems.[9] In a letter to the racist author Earnest Sevier Cox, Carto complained about the "N*ggerfication of America."[10] Fearing this "n*ggerfication," Carto organized the Joint Council for Repatriation, which advocated the return of all Blacks to Africa.

In a 1989 interview, Weber told the *University of Nebraska Sower* that he feared the United States was becoming "a sort of Mexicanized, Puertoricanized country," due to the failure of White Americans to reproduce adequately.[11] Brandon's successor as IHR director, Tom Marcellus, has criticized acceptance of the Holocaust "hoax" on the ground that it does damage to the "self-image of White people."[12]

Predictably, prominent members of the Ku Klux Klan are also Holocaust deniers. In the *Crusader,* the publication of David Duke's organization, the National Association for the Advancement of White People, Duke termed the Holocaust a "historical hoax."[13] These words of a former Grand Wizard of the KKK highlight the affinities between Holocaust denial and classical

American racism (an association that may appropriately be pointed out by teachers in the classroom).

Admiration for the white supremacist doctrines advocated by Hitler is also visible among prominent foreign deniers of the Holocaust. For example, Ernst Zundel, a German citizen with immigrant status in Canada, has advanced the claim that Jews were not killed in the gas chambers. Zundel is the author of the book *The Hitler We Loved and Why*, which praises Hitler and his white supremacist ideology.[14] Zundel has no academic credentials relevant to the study of the Holocaust.

Among the "soft" deniers is David Irving, a British popular historian (the only well-known denier with a knowledge of history, though without adequate academic historical credentials). Irving argues that about 500,000 to 600,000 Jews died as victims of war,[15] and claims that Hitler did not know about the Final Solution. His view of Hitler is reflected, according to Lipstadt, by his having "placed a self-portrait of Hitler over his desk," and having described his visit to Hitler's mountaintop retreat as a "spiritual experience."[16] In 1994, David Irving stated "I think the Jews are largely to blame for themselves by the knee-jerk responses [to anti-Semitism]... Goebbels himself said that, in fact."[17]

Combating the Denial of the Holocaust in the Classroom

Denial is a position contrary to the facts, and should not be treated by teachers as a matter of opinion representing one side of a debate. The most effective way to deal with the deniers is for teachers to thoroughly learn, and then teach, the storyline of the Holocaust. An extraordinary amount of Holocaust documentation exists, enabling teachers to eliminate arguments of denial by citing the facts and sharing their awareness of the documentation with students.

The Scale of Documentation

Due to the nature of German record keeping, the Holocaust is one of the more thoroughly documented historical events in the annals of humanity. For example, at the World War II Records Division of the National Archives in Alexandria, Virginia, Holocaust related material fills 28,000 linear feet of shelves. This includes mostly military documents, some SS documents, and some documents of the civil administration. And here we are only speaking of the Holocaust material in a single location.

Documentation of the Holocaust exists all over the world. There are hundreds of thousands of orders, decrees, memos, letters, blueprints, and memoirs. Eyewitness testimonies abound. There are graphic photographs and clips of documentary footage, taken by both military officials and civilians, of atrocities such as the *Einsatzgruppen* (Mobile Killing Units) shootings. Particularly dramatic is the testimony of the Nazis themselves. The major perpetrators of the Nazi crimes, on trial at Nuremberg, did not deny that the Holocaust took place, though they did try to place the blame for it on other Nazis.

Contrary to popular belief, there is an abundance of material dealing with the gas chambers. Many believe that since the Nazis themselves destroyed the gas chambers and crematoria (out of fear of retribution), there remains no evidence of the gas chambers. However, documentation exists. For example, remains of the gas chambers were found at the Auschwitz-Birkenau and Majdanek death camps (at Majdanek, in fact, not all the gas chambers were destroyed). Blueprints of the gas chambers exist in the archives at the Auschwitz Museum as well as in Moscow, and now in the archives at the Research Institute of the U.S. Holocaust Memorial Museum in Washington, D.C. There are Allied aerial photographs of the crematoria, as well as clandestine photographs of the crematoria and of people walking to the gas chambers. Deniers claim that the gas chambers were only used for delousing. But even the commandant of Auschwitz, Rudolf Hoess, made no attempt to deny the gas chambers. In his autobiography, Hoess described the gassing process:

> Then, very quickly, the door was hermetically sealed, and a can of gas was immediately thrown onto the floor, through an

opening ... in the ceiling of the gas chamber, by the disinfectors, who were standing ready. This led to the immediate release of the gas ... those who were near the opening died immediately ... a third died within a moment. The others began to struggle, to scream, to choke ... after a few minutes all were on the ground. After a maximum of twenty minutes, nobody moved.[18]

Other testimony comes from camp guards and from survivors of Auschwitz (members of the *Sonderkommando* - Jewish prisoners assigned to work at the crematoria). In the case of the Belzec and Sobibor death camps, as well as at Auschwitz-Birkenau, a vast quantity of gassing victims' shoes, clothing and other personal belongings was discovered by Soviet soldiers at the war's end. At the liberation of Auschwitz-Birkenau, Soviet troops also found over 15,000 pounds of human hair. Other documents record the ordering and supply of Zyklon-B gas.

Much of the written documentation on the Holocaust is now available in English, and is useful for teachers. Raul Hilberg, this country's pre-eminent historian of the Holocaust, has collected much of this material in *Documents of Destruction*. Hilberg also documents decrees and deportations in his momentous *The Destruction of the European Jews*. John Mendelsohn has published an eighteen-volume compendium of Holocaust documentation entitled *The Holocaust*. Daily accounts by German army officers of mass shootings of Jews and others, as well as lists of areas made *judenrein*, "cleansed of Jews," have been translated into English as *The Einsatzgruppen Reports*. Danuta Czech's *Auschwitz Chronicle* (805 pages), is now available in English. It contains the Nazi daily records of Auschwitz down to the smallest details- construction of gas chambers, deportations, arrival numbers and numbers gassed. Perhaps the best overview of operations at Auschwitz is the newly released *Anatomy of the Auschwitz Death Camp*, edited by Michael Berenbaum and Yisrael Gutman.[19]

Also available in English are the proceedings of the Nuremberg and other post-war trials.[20] These are an extraordinarily useful tool in verifying the historicity of the Holocaust, because here the perpetrators of the crime gave first-hand evidence. Unlike today's Holocaust deniers, the perpetrators never denied that the crime took place. Some tried to justify their actions by expressing their fear of Jews; some claimed "orders from above," while others acknowledged what happened while claiming that others did the actual killing. But never did they deny the Holocaust. As Hilberg concludes "... there was no denial obviously among any of the people who were in any way even close to these [killing] operations- no denial in the railways, no denial in the finance ministry, no denial in the SS, and so on and so forth."[21] Should students request that the "Nazi point of view" be taught, the testimonies of the perpetrators offer the best answer to such a request.

Inquisitive students will no doubt ask whether any of the many historical documents on the Holocaust have been forged. Unlike some other major historical phenomena, the study of the Holocaust has not faced the problem of false documents. In an interview by Michael Berenbaum, director of the Holocaust Museum's Research Institute, Hilberg states that he has never in his "45 more years of research in this field found a forged document."[22] Students may need to be shown that forgery of historical documents is somewhat more sophisticated than the kind of forgery students may know from personal experience. As Hilberg points out:

> It sounds easy, but it is very, very difficult if one were to attempt it. For one thing, it is a matter of the right paper, the right typewriter, but even more, it is the proper language. One would have to be extraordinarily knowledgeable about the nature of the administrative operations to be able to feign the document and put it as though if it were real...[23]

Forgery on the enormous scale of the Holocaust documentation would be impossible. The documents are too numerous, their sources too diverse, and the time period of their discovery too limited for such massive, coordinated forgery to take place. And there was no conceivable reason for the discoverers of most documents, the victorious World War II Allies, to fabricate the vast quantity of documents about the Holocaust.

A Key Resource: The Holocaust Museum

In the United States, the most thorough pedagogical documentation of the Holocaust, which presents the historical timeline of the Holocaust from beginning to end, is the United States Holocaust Memorial Museum in Washington, D.C.[24] Almost all the contents of the Museum's permanent exhibition are actual artifacts-objects, photos, oral histories, eyewitness evidence, including the testimony of survivors, and documentary footage. These objects tell a story, a history of the Holocaust, from its beginning through its middle to its end making, the Museum an important pedagogical tool.[25] Though the purpose of the Holocaust Museum is to teach a lesson and preserve memory, and not to answer the claims of those who say the event never happened, the institution ends up doing this as well.

Inscribed on the walls of the building and repeated at the beginning of the Museum's permanent exhibition are the words of General Eisenhower after witnessing the Ohrdruf concentration camp following its liberation—the first publicized testimony by an American on the atrocities of the Holocaust:

> The things I saw beggar description ... the visual evidence and verbal testimony of starvation, cruelty and bestiality were overpowering...I made the visit deliberately in order to be in a position to give first-hand evidence of these things if ever, in the future, there develops a tendency to charge these allegations to propaganda.[26]

Adding to the pedagogical and documentary value of the Museum is the Wexner Learning Center, a multi-media center where visitors can access, on a single screen, various media of original documentation on the Holocaust-documentary footage, photos, survivors and eyewitness testimonies, music, maps and a daily Holocaust chronology.

Teachers at the high school level can take advantage of the various archival collections of the Holocaust Museum's scholarly division-the United States Holocaust Research Institute. The Institute's archive consists of a Documents Archive, Photo Archive,

Oral History Archive, Film and Video Archive, Library, and Registry of Jewish Holocaust Survivors. The notion of "archives" should not be treated as an unfriendly concept by classroom educators. The access to primary sources that they provide offers teachers at all levels a major opportunity.

A notable resource of the Research Institute is its especially rich archival collection of materials from Eastern Europe, Germany, and the former U.S.S.R. Much of the material captured by the Red Army in 1945, and then sequestered for forty-five years in Soviet archives, has been made available to western scholars with the dissolution of the Communist bloc. A significant part of this material is in the Research Institute's archives, making it one of the largest repositories of Holocaust documentation.

The Education Department of the Museum also offers teacher training workshops for educators wishing to incorporate the Holocaust into their curricula, and a teacher's Resource Center, equipped with teaching guides arranged according to specific topics, e.g. ghettos, camps, etc. and various media useful for Holocaust education. During the two years since the museum's opening, the Resource Center has responded to more than 70,000 requests from educators.

Conclusion

Teachers can teach the Holocaust by utilizing all the objective sources and scientific methodologies appropriate for teaching history. The singularity of the Final Solution in human history makes it an emotional subject, but emotion and historicity are not mutually exclusive. As with other historical events, the Holocaust has had its share of historiographical debates. The facts about the Holocaust are not, however, a matter of debate, and teachers need not hesitate to point out the racist ideologies and lack of academic credentials of deniers of the Holocaust. In the words of Deborah Lipstadt, truth does not have to "be on the defensive." [27]

Notes

1 Perhaps the best known case of a claim that Jews were never gassed was that of Fred Leuchter, a self-described engineer from Massachusetts (Leuchter has no engineering credentials). Leuchter spent three days at Auschwitz and one in Majdanek to determine whether systematic gassing occurred there. Upon his return, he published his finding in *The Leuchter Report: An Engineering Report on the Alleged Execution Gas Chambers at Auschwitz, Birkenau, and Majdanek, Poland*. Leuchter based his finding on "forensic samples" he gathered while inspecting the remains of the gas chambers. His findings were dismissed by engineers, historians, and officials of the State Museum at Auschwitz.

2 There are revisionist schools on some of the major historical events of this century. Among the best-known are those on the origins and outcomes of World War I and the Cold War. However, the revisionist schools revise the traditional historiography of these events. They interpret, but do not deny, the fact of their existence.

3 Deborah Lipstadt, *Denying The Holocaust: The Growing Assault on Truth and Memory* (New York: Free Press, 1993).

4 Ibid., 146.

5 Ibid. Cited in Richard Harwood's 28-page booklet *Did Six Million Really Die? The Truth At Last.*

6 Ibid., 144.

7 Cited by Lipstadt from John C. Obert, "Yockey: Profile of an American Hitler," *The Investigator* (Oct. 1981): 8.8Ibid., 13

8. As a result of his "racist politics," Brandon (McCalden) was denied membership into the English National Union of Journalists.

9 Ibid., 146.

10 Ibid.

11 Cited in Michael Shermer, "Proving the Holocaust: The Refutation of Revisionism and the Restoration of History," in *Skeptic* 2, no. 4 (1994).

12 Lipstadt, *Denying The Holocaust*, 143.

13 In l986, David Duke, who denied that Jews were killed in the gas chambers, declared that "Jews deserve to go into the ash bin of history." Jason Berry, "Duke's Disguise." *The New York Times*, Oct. 19, 1991.

14 Lipstadt, 158. Zundel established a publishing house, Samisdat Publications, which has reprinted and distributed anti-Semitic and racist literature.

15 David Irving, *Hitler's War* (New York: Viking Press, 1977).

16 Cited in Robert Harris, *Selling Hitler* (New York: 1986)

17 Ibid.

18 Rudolf Hoess, *Commandant of Auschwitz: The Autobiography of Rudolf Hoess*, (Cleveland: World Press, 1959), 166. Hoess was arrested in 1946. In the

Krakow jail where he was held, Hoess wrote an autobiography in which he described the implementation of the Final Solution. At the Hoess trial, held before a Polish war crimes tribunal from March 11 to 29, 1947, the sending of Jews to the gas chambers was reconstructed by Hoess's testimony.

19 Raul Hilberg (ed.), *Documents of Destruction* (London: W.H. Allen, 1972); John Mendelsohn (ed.), *The Holocaust: Selected Documents in Eighteen Volumes* (New York: Garland Publishing, 1982); Y. Arad, S. Krakowski, S. Spector (eds), *Einsatzgruppen Reports* (New York: Holocaust Library, 1989); Danuta Czech (ed.), *Auschwitz Chronicle* (New York: H. Holt, 1990); Michael Berenbaum and Yisrael Gutman (eds.), *Anatomy of the Auschwitz Death Camp* (Bloomington: Indiana University Press, 1994).

20 Publications on the postwar trials, including the minutes of the Nuremberg and other trials of major war criminals, as well as secondary accounts, are widely available in public and university libraries. Documentary footage of the Nuremberg and other postwar trials, notably the Eichmann trial, is also available. One outstanding published source on the Nuremberg trials is International Military Tribunal, *The Trial of the Major War Criminals Before the International Military Tribunal, Blue Series* (Nuremberg: 42 volumes, 1947-1949).

21 "What Do We Know About the Holocaust," interview with Raul Hilberg. Conducted by Michael Berenbaum, Director, United States Holocaust Research Institute (of the United States Holocaust Memorial Museum), February 1994.

22 Ibid. Berenbaum interview with Hilberg.

23 Ibid.

24 The Holocaust Museum opened in April 1993. It has since had approximately three million visitors. According to a survey, over 60% of the visitors are not Jewish.

25 Following a 1980 Congressional vote mandating the establishment of a memorial in Washington, D.C. to all the victims of the Holocaust, it was initially decided to build a "memoriaquot; in the Washington sense of the word-a monument. This posed a pedagogical problem. One does not learn a complete story, or any story, from a monument. Monuments memorialize stories that are already known. The story of the Holocaust was not known to the majority of Americans. Therefore, it was decided, for pedagogical reasons, to build a chronological exhibit to document the story of the Holocaust.

26 Eisenhower visited the site of Ohrdruf concentration camp on April 4, 1945. See Judah Nadich, Eisenhower and the Jews (New York: Twayne Publishers, 1953). Eisenhower's statement is an illustration of the fact that much documentation of the Holocaust is from American and other Allied sources. Much of the documentation is currently in American archives, such as the National Archives in Washington, D.C.

27 "What Do We Know About Holocaust Denial." Interview conducted by the author with Deborah Lipstadt, February 1994. This interview was conducted as part of an effort by the Research Institute of the United States Holocaust Memorial Museum to educate university students with the facts on Holocaust denial. This effort was in response to a string of advertisements by Holocaust deniers which

Should Holocaust Denial Be Legal?

were printed in university newspapers throughout the country in l994. In addition to an interview with Lipstadt, students receive an interview with Raul Hilberg and a letter from Walter Rockler, a leading attorney and prosecutor at Nuremberg Trials, who demonstrates that the printing of denial ads is not a civil liberties issue. Newspapers are under no obligation to take money to publish the opinions of racists.

Laws Are Not an Effective Means of Addressing Holocaust Denial

Timothy Garton Ash

Timothy Garton Ash is a historian and columnist with the Guardian.

The German justice minister has proposed that all EU states should criminalise Holocaust denial and ban the public display of Nazi insignia, as Germany itself does. The EU's justice commissioner has apparently supported her. No reasonable person will doubt their good intentions, but this would be a big mistake. I hope and trust that other EU members will put a stop to this deeply unwise proposal, as they have to similar ones in the past.

Let me be clear about my starting-point. The Nazi Holocaust of the European Jews was unique. The main historical facts about it should be known by every contemporary European. Trying to ensure that nothing like that ever again happens here in Europe (or anywhere else in the world, insofar as that is in our power) should be one of the fundamental aims of the EU. As someone who came to European affairs through the study of Nazi Germany, I can say that this was a major reason for my personal commitment to what we call the European project.

That a measure is well-intended does not, however, make it wise. The road to hell is paved with good intentions. And this proposal is very unwise. First of all, if passed, it would further curtail free expression—at a time when that is under threat from many quarters. Free expression is a unique and primary good in free societies; it's the oxygen that sustains other freedoms. You must therefore have very good reasons for restricting it by law.

The German justice minister, Brigitte Zypries, argues that she has such reasons. Recalling the way in which the anti-semitic words

The agreed upon 1,239 words from A Blanket Ban on Holocaust Denial Would be a Serious Mistake *by Timothy Garton Ash. Published by The Guardian, 2007. © Timothy Garton Ash. Reproduced by permission of the author c/o Rogers, Coleridge & White Ltd., 20 Powis Mews, London W11 1JN.*

of Hitler and others paved the way for the horrors of Nazism, she says: "This historical experience puts Germany under a permanent obligation to combat systematically every form of racism, anti-semitism and xenophobia. And we should not wait until it comes to deeds. We must act already against the intellectual pathbreakers of the crime" (I translate from a speech posted on the German justice ministry's website). So this additional restriction on free expression—an EU-wide ban on Holocaust denial and Nazi insignia—is justified because it will make a significant difference to combating racism, anti-semitism and xenophobia today.

But what is the evidence for that? Nine EU member states currently have laws against Holocaust denial: Austria, Belgium, the Czech Republic, France, Germany, Lithuania, Poland, Romania and Slovakia. That happens to be a list of countries with some of the strongest rightwing xenophobic parties in the EU, from France's National Front and the Vlaams Belang in Belgium to the NPD in Germany and the Greater Romania party. Self-evidently those parties don't exist as a result of Holocaust denial laws. Indeed, the existence of such parties is one of the reasons given for having the laws, but the laws have obviously not prevented their vigorous and dangerous growth. If anything, the bans and resulting court cases have given them a nimbus of persecution, that far-right populists love to exploit.

The same thing has happened with the imprisonment of David Irving in Austria. Six years ago Irving lost, in the British high court, a spectacular libel case that he had himself initiated against the American historian Deborah Lipstadt, who had described him as "one of the most prominent and dangerous Holocaust deniers." Mr Justice Gray concluded that Irving was "an active Holocaust denier." The last shreds of his reputation as a serious historian were torn apart—in a country that does not ban Holocaust denial. Now, having served time in Austria for statements he made there 16 years before, he can pose as a martyr for free speech and receives renewed publicity for his calumnies. At a press conference after his release,

Holocaust Deniers and Conspiracy Theorists

he reportedly endorsed the drunken anti-semitic comment of Mel Gibson that "the Jews" are responsible for all the wars in the world

Now suppose the ban on displaying Nazi insignia had already been in force EU-wide and the British courts had therefore been obliged to prosecute Prince Harry for (offensively and idiotically) sporting an Afrika Korps uniform and swastika armband at a friend's fancy dress party. What would that have done to combat Eurosceptic and xenophobic extremism in Britain? Nothing. Quite the reverse: it would have been worth thousands of votes to the British National party. And while we're on the subject of the swastika, Hindus across Europe are protesting against the proposed ban, on the grounds that for them the swastika is an ancient symbol of peace. Meanwhile, the German legal authorities have got themselves into a ridiculous tangle because a court in Stuttgart has convicted the manager of a mail-order company for selling T-shirts showing crossed-out and crushed swastikas. These might be anti-fascist T-shirts, you see, but they still showed swastikas and were therefore illegal. And so it goes on, and would go on even more if the whole EU adopted such measures.

The argument that these well-intentioned bans actually feed the flames they are meant to quench is, of course, ultimately unprovable, although circumstantial and anecdotal evidence points in that direction. But the burden of proof is on the proponents of the ban. In a free society, any restriction on free speech must have a compelling justification - and that is not available here.

Holocaust denial should be combated in our schools, our universities and our media, not in police stations and courts. It is, at most, a minor contributing factor to today's far-right racism and xenophobia, which now mainly targets Muslims, people of different skin colour, and migrants of all kinds. Nor will today's anti-semitism be countered most effectively by such bans; they may, at the margins, even stoke it up, feeding conspiracy theories about Jewish power and accusations of double-standards. Citizens of the Baltic states, who suffered so terribly under Stalin, will ask why only denial of the Holocaust should be criminalised and not denial of the gulag. Armenians will add: and why not the genocide that our ancestors experienced at the hands of the Turks? And Muslims: why not cartoons of Muhammad?

The approach advocated by the German justice minister also reeks of the nanny state. It speaks in the name of freedom but does not trust people to exercise freedom responsibly. Citizens are to be treated as children, guided and guarded at every turn. Indeed, the more I look at what Zypries does and says, the more she seems to me the personification of the contemporary European nanny state. It's no accident that she has also been closely involved in extending German law to allow more bugging of private homes. Vertrauen ist gut, Kontrolle ist besser (trust is good, control is better). Isn't that another mistake Germany made in the past?

Zypries is right: we must learn the lessons of history. But we must learn the right lessons of history, the ones relevant to a free, multicultural continent today. "Experience shows," writes the former attorney general of India, Soli Sorabjee, "that criminal laws prohibiting hate speech and expression will encourage intolerance, divisiveness and unreasonable interference with freedom of expression ... We need not more repressive laws but more free speech to combat bigotry and to promote tolerance." True for India and true for Europe.

Laws Banning Holocaust Denial Are at Odds with the Constitution and Free Speech

Kenneth Lasson

Kenneth Lasson is a professor at the University of Baltimore School of Law.

From the ashes of the Holocaust we have come once again to learn the terrible truth, that the power of Evil cannot be underestimated.

Nor can the effect of the spoken and written word. It has been but a half-century since the liberation of Nazi death camps, a little more than a decade since the First International Conference on the Holocaust and Human Rights, and a few short years since the United States Holocaust Memorial Museum first put on display its documentation of horror. Yet today that form of historical revisionism popularly called "Holocaust denial" abounds worldwide in all its full foul flourish. As the generation of survivors dwindles, whose words will win?

In a global environment increasingly dominated by mass media of manifold form and format, we have also begun to understand that what is printed on paper or broadcast on television or bytten into cyberspace affects everyone, actually or subliminally. Conversely, what is rejected or otherwise left out is doomed to the World of Communication Failure or, worse, of Ignorance and Misunderstanding.

Who decides what is to appear in the vast and burgeoning marketplace of ideas? Many of those important choices are vested in editors and publishers, upon whom the Constitution confers almost unfettered discretion. Restrictions are few and seldom imposed; for the most part journalists can write, say, depict—or ignore—just

"Holocaust Denial and the First Amendment: The Quest for Truth in a Free Society," by Kenneth Lasson, University of Baltimore School of Law, https://scholarworks.law.ubalt.edu/cgi/viewcontent.cgi?article=1383&context=all_fac. Reprinted by permission.

about anything they want. And that's the way we like it. That's the American way. Freedom of thought and expression, after all, is one of our most hallowed liberties-limited only by circumstances where actual harm has been caused or is reasonably perceived as imminent. If a line can be drawn at all between unfair suppression of thought on the one hand and good editorial judgment on the other, it is sometimes exceedingly faint, often entirely arbitrary, and always fundamentally subjective. The greater the opportunity for excess in the exercise of the power of the press, the more profoundly difficult the consequences in the protection of civil liberties for individuals.

That axiom has been brought into sharp focus by Holocaust deniers, whose goal is both enhanced and complicated by the aura of "political correctness" which nowadays surrounds a great deal of editorial decision-making. Nowhere is this more pervasive than in Academia. What should be the most receptive place for honest intellectual inquiry and discourse has instead become one where all assumptions are open to debate—even documented historical facts. This has had an unsettling effect on student editors, who have long been responsive to the pressures of political correctness. When they become entangled in the black and nefarious thickets of Holocaust denial, their exercise of editorial discretion can be intellectually excruciating.

So can the emotional pain suffered by victims of group libel. Remedies for that malady have not been clearly established in American law. Nor has the tort of intentional infliction of emotional distress been adequately tested against traditional free-speech guarantees. Explored least of all is the effect upon a free society when the dissemination of demonstrably false ideas is Constitutionally protected.

Must writers and speakers who deny the Holocaust be guaranteed equal access to curricula and classrooms? Should responsible libraries collect and classify work born of blatant bigotry? Have survivors been injured when their victimization has been repudiated?

More profoundly, can we reject spurious revisionism, or punish purposeful expressions of hatred, and still pay homage to the liberty of thought ennobled by the First Amendment? Should the People have the power to suppress the misrepresentation of historical fact when it is motivated by nothing more than racial animus? Are some conflicts between freedom of expression and civility as insoluble as they are inevitable? Can history ever be proven as Truth?

This Article attempts to answer those questions.

Holocaust Denial

Nazis, Nuremberg, and the Origins of Revisionism

The Nazis themselves recognized that the incredibility of what they had done would cast shadows of doubt upon any eyewitness reports. Inmates at concentration camps testified that they were frequently taunted by their captors: "And even if some proof should remain and some of you survive, people will say that the events you describe are too monstrous to be believed; they will say that they are the exaggerations of Allied propaganda and will believe us, who will deny everything, and not you."

Early newspaper accounts of the camps were obscured by dispatches about the war's progress, if not indeed questioned for their veracity. That is why after the Nazis were conquered, every American soldier not committed to the front lines was ordered to visit the death camps, so as to bear witness to places like Auschwitz, Belsen, and Buchenwald. It likewise explains why the Nuremberg Tribunal was so intent on documenting all of the atrocities found by the Allied liberators. "The things I saw beggar description," said General Dwight D. Eisenhower in a statement now etched in stone at the entrance to the U.S. Holocaust Memorial Museum in Washington, D.C. "I made the visit deliberately, in order to be in a position to give first-hand evidence of these things if ever, in the future, there develops a tendency to charge these allegations merely to propaganda."

Alas, Eisenhower understated the possibilities. In recent years, the contention that there was no mass extermination of Jews and no deaths in gas chambers at the hands of the Nazis has given rise to a nasty and pervasive (if predictable) cottage industry. Holocaust-denial books have made their way into university and public libraries across the country and around the world.

Revisionists have also taken to late-night public-access television to assert that claims of Nazi genocide against the Jews during World War II are part of an elaborate hoax. Slickly produced videos purport to show that concentration camps like Auschwitz and Birkenau were recreational facilities, not death camps. Holocaust deniers claim that archival materials concerning Nazi atrocities-voluminously detailed lists of victims, miles of gruesome film footage, and vividly remembered accounts of eyewitnesses- have all been forged.

Meanwhile, as use of the computer Internet has burgeoned, its millions of subscribers provide a vast new target audience for the efforts of numerous hate groups. Catering to white supremacists, anti-government survivalists, militiamen and would-be terrorists, Holocaust deniers have set up enough new sites on the World Wide Web to reach a larger potential constituency than any revolutionaries in history.

[…]

First Amendment Considerations
Principles of Liberty
Ben Franklin's view may have been civil and proper, but the Founding Fathers were motivated by a much more libertarian philosophy when they drafted the Bill of Rights. The First Amendment not only protects media from government interference, but grants the press almost absolute power to print whatever it wishes. Freedom of the press, often characterized as "the mother of all our liberties," had "little or nothing to do with truth-telling. . . . Most of the early newspapers were partisan sheets devoted to attacks on political opponents. . . . " Back then, freedom of the press meant "the right to be just or unjust, partisan or non-partisan, true or false, in news column or editorial column." That

same freedom also allows newspapers to reject any matter, editorial or advertising.

[...]

The Right of Access

Regardless (or because) of interpretations of the Framers' intent, clear law has evolved around the right of access to newspapers, limitations on government interference with them, and the characterization of public forums.

While for the most part individuals may be guaranteed freedom from government regulation of their privately-owned presses, citizens have never had the right of access to someone else's printed pages The Constitution does not grant a print forum to those without the wherewithal to start up their own newspapers, nor has Congress.

Is there any difference between the First Amendment rights afforded a privately-owned commercial newspaper and one sponsored by a private college or university? Is a public college or university newspaper any less protected by the Constitution?

Since newspapers have limited publishing space (and funds), editors must use their subjective judgment on a regular basis to determine exactly what will be published and what will not. A paper may refuse to print certain editorial material because of its content or due to lack of space or, in the case of advertising, out of financial considerations. While rejection based on space or financial considerations does not constitute an infringement on free speech, a content-based rejection may. The constitutionality of editorial discretion depends on the status of the publication-that is, whether it is an instrumentality of the state (in the language of the law, a "state actor"), or is privately owned, funded, and operated.

Editors always make choices about what to publish, nurturing a bond of trust between them and their readers. That trust is violated if they knowingly disseminate historical lies like Holocaust-denial advertisements. With the power to publish comes the responsibility to seek truth, as well as to avoid defamatory propaganda.

Over two decades ago the Supreme Court held that a private newspaper had a constitutional right to determine whether or not to publish a specific article, editorial, or advertisement. In *Miami Herald Publ'g Co. v. Tornillo*, the Court rejected a Florida statute requiring newspapers to publish replies to political editorials. Its decision was based upon the First Amendment's guarantee of freedom of the press and freedom of speech. As Chief Justice Burger wrote for the Court, "the clear implication [of precedent] has been that any . . . compulsion to publish that which 'reason' tells [editors] should not be published is unconstitutional."

In essence, the Court held that editorial discretion under the First Amendment is almost absolute. Newspapers have a right to publish or refuse to publish whatever they choose-articles, editorials, or advertisements. Even if the newspaper is the only one in town, or the biggest, or the most widely read, it can still print or reject practically anything. That an individual or group has the wherewithal to pay for an advertisement does not guarantee access to a newspaper owned or operated by others. It can even discriminate against a particular advertiser if it so desires. In the absence of fraud or monopoly "it is immaterial whether such [discrimination] is based upon reason or is the result of mere caprice, prejudice or malice. It is a part of the liberty of action which the Constitutions, State and Federal, guarantee to the citizen."

Although privately owned and operated newspapers are by no means state actors, their First Amendment freedoms are not absolute. True, prior restraints are seldom countenanced under the Constitution—the rare exceptions relate to the publication of editorial matter advocating acts likely to incite imminent lawless action or disclosing state secrets—but newspapers may be punished after the fact for publishing libelous or obscene material. Thus private commercial newspapers may be prohibited from publishing information deemed damaging to national security and exhortations to violence or civil disobedience, and punished for publishing defamatory stories and material considered obscene.

In balance, though, privately owned and operated newspapers have virtually unfettered discretion about what to publish, and what not to publish. Just as editors are free to print almost anything, so can they decide what to reject. While the public might have a moral claim to have opinions expressed on editorial pages, it has no constitutional right of access to them.

[…]

The Dangers of Censorship

Few Americans want the government to decide for them what they can hear on the street corner, read in the library, or see in the cinema. It is not difficult to find abuses in the name of fair play, especially in countries which (unlike the United States) permit censorship and criminalization of that which the government finds to be hate speech.

Criminalization illustrates the difficulties of line-drawing. For example, the distinguished historian Bernard Lewis was recently found guilty, in Paris, France, of expressing doubts that the massacre of 1.5 million Armenians early in this century by the Ottoman Empire could be correctly termed a "genocide."

In Germany, a relatively recent law makes it a crime to deny the Holocaust "or another violent and arbitrary dominance." This clause became quite contentious, the resulting controversy centering around the issues of restricting historical facts, promoting national consciousness, attributing collective guilt, and identifying the role of courts in punishing lies. Should denial of the violent expulsion of Germans from Soviet-occupied East Germany be punishable? In other words, was the Holocaust a unique phenomenon?

If Auschwitz is unique, the argument goes, then the clause "or another violent and arbitrary dominance" should have been eliminated; this addition renders the Holocaust unjustifiably relative, and offends both the memory of those murdered and the sensibilities of survivors.

In addition, the experience with earlier legislation shows that hate- speech defendants, almost without exception, remain convinced if not strengthened in the truth of their contentions. Not only is deterrence unlikely, there is a real danger of backlash. The lie is forbidden but liars remain. The judicial process cannot carry the burden of education that should fall to family, school, and political discourse. To the contrary, the German courts have become forums for neo-Nazi propaganda.

Moreover, the task of drawing a line between "good" and "bad" is exceedingly difficult. Every year in the United States, various books are banned by public libraries. They have included everything from Thomas Paine's *The Age of Reason* and John Steinbeck's *The Grapes of Wrath* to Charles Darwin's *On the Origin of the Species* and the King James version of the *Holy Bible*. In recent years the growing influence of the religious right has been reflected in challenges to books about the occult, homosexuals, and racial minorities.

In Canada, customs officials issue a list of imported materials that are reviewed for their potential to stir up racial hatred. Of the ninety titles on a recent list, only four were banned, including: the standard anti-Semitic text, *The Protocols of the Elders of Zion*; Henry Ford's *The International Jew: The World's Foremost Problem*; and Arthur Butz's *The Hoax of the Twentieth Century*. Those that were not banned included *An Empire of Their Own: How Jews Invented Hollywood and Aryan Outlaws in a Zionist Police State*.

There is little evidence that banning hate speech and literature serves to inhibit it. On the other hand, line-drawing has proven all but impossible.

[…]

Using Laws to Shape Historical Memory Can Have Sinister Consequences

Eric Heinze

Eric Heinze is a professor of law at Queen Mary University of London.

The Lithuanian capital Vilnius has a public monument honouring the US rock star Frank Zappa. To place the statue in a prominent public space required a special law to be passed in 1992. It was seen as a deliberate symbol of the country's break from its Soviet-bloc past, the remnants of which were being swept away—including statues of Communist era heroes such as Lenin and Stalin.

Was this a frivolous use of law? Sure, it was deliberately eccentric—yet all nations use law in one way or another to mould collective understandings of the past.

The Vilnius law happens to stand at a rather extreme end of what law is and does. After all, there's no obvious way one can violate it. It's certainly not the kind of law that punishes anyone for doing anything. A judge might slap a fine on you for defacing the monument, but that is true of most property, public or private, whether it's the bust of a rock star, the door of a local tax office, or your neighbour's grinning garden gnome.

If we swing to the opposite extreme, the use of law to shape popular historical memory suddenly becomes bleaker. Systemic executions and labour-camp imprisonment of whole families threaten any North Korean who openly challenges the state's official history.

A particular group of laws—as old as law itself, yet only recently studied as a distinct type—can be called "memory laws." They

---

"Law can enshrine a country's history, but it is a citizen's right to question it," by Eric Heinze, The Conversation, May 19, 2016, https://theconversation.com/law-can-enshrine-a-countrys-history-but-it-is-a-citizens-right-to-question-it-59561. Licensed under CC BY-ND 4.0 International.

Should Holocaust Denial Be Legal?

embody the countless ways in which nations use law to mould popular understandings of history.

As we probe the Vilnius law more closely, it turns out to be less whimsical than it might at first appear. The sculpture overtly satirises a chilling past, when ubiquitous, taboo-laden images of state-approved heroes had been planted throughout Soviet-dominated nations. During the Cold War, such "art" could be ridiculed only in whispers.

The lesson is one we must learn forever anew: a government's legitimacy is reflected in the degree to which it tolerates its citizens lampooning and deriding it. Lithuanians have today gained the freedom to detest Zappa the man as loudly as they wish, along with any understandings of history that his image memorialises.

To be sure, not all Lithuanian laws and practices are equally enlightened. Pandering to local post-Soviet nationalism, the state has brought a few nasty prosecutions against elderly Holocaust survivors on trumped-up charges of wartime collaboration.

Still, in a curious way, the Zappa display shows at its very best how a government can use law to promote a view of the past. The monument exists precisely to invite responses openly critical of any state-approved history.

Passionate Debates

Along that spectrum from Vilnius to Pyongyang, states devise countless ways to inscribe their preferred versions of history into law—not only of their own past, but of any number of historical events.

In several countries—Switzerland, for example—it is illegal to openly deny the Armenian Genocide. Those laws have been challenged, however, on grounds of free speech. Meanwhile Turkey has prosecuted citizens who question state policies denying that any genocide occurred, notably the novelist Orhan Pamuk.

The fact that European standards governing the Nazi and the Turkish genocides often differ has sparked furious debates. The denial of the Jewish Holocaust is treated differently by European states—because, according to some, of Europe's closer ties to it.

Even if we accept that distinction, however, European laws are scarcely unanimous. Many Germans passionately support laws against Holocaust denial, while Britain looks sceptically on imposing criminal penalties as a means for structuring either popular or academic discussions.

Human Rights

The use of law to shape historical memory is sometimes benign, then, and yet sometimes atrocious. But despite the vast range of memory laws, from silly to solemn to sinister, what unites them is that states rarely bother with law for non-contentious histories. So perhaps the best way to judge a state's overall attitude towards human rights is to observe its attitude towards history.

We may certainly question, for example, the wisdom of Holocaust denial laws in states such as Germany or Switzerland. But what stands out in such democracies is that those laws are the exception that prove the rule—in general these countries admit the most relentless scrutiny of their pasts and their politics. At the same time they are states with, if not impeccable, certainly solid records within the post-World War II systems of international human rights.

That's no coincidence. There are vital human rights, such as prohibitions on torture or guarantees of a fair trial—to which many states further add rights to minimum levels of food, clothing, shelter, education, or employment. Yet it is an error to see free expression about controversial issues as "just another right" on a "checklist" of human rights. The fundamental attitude necessary for a state to secure human rights is an attitude inviting no-holds-barred criticism of its actions both present and past.

That is what memory laws reveal. If you want to know where a state's ethical compass lies, if you want to know its attitude towards human rights, then yes, look by all means at its official version of past events—but look above all at the freedom of its citizens to challenge that version.

Those Who Deny the Holocaust Are Denying History and in Some Countries Face Legal Consequences

Volker Wagener

Volker Wagener is a journalist and opinion writer at Deutsche Welle.

She is 87 years old, and she refuses to learn. Ursula Haverbeck is well-known in legal circles all over Germany. She's been keeping the courts busy for years: in the Westphalian town of Detmold; in Verden near Bremen; in Hamburg; in Berlin; and Tuesday (October 11) in another Westphalian town, Bad Oeynhausen. Again and again public prosecutors have had to investigate accusations of incitement made against her. This sprightly old lady is popular in far-right political circles. She denies the Holocaust, and even at her advanced age is able to provoke uproar in the courtroom.

In February this year she tried to enter the courtroom in Detmold during the trial of a former Auschwitz SS guard. As far as she's concerned, Auschwitz was just a labor camp, not an extermination camp. She insists that the Nazi genocide of the Jews is "the biggest and most sustained lie in history." Ursula Haverbeck is not the most high-profile example of denial of Nazi Germany's crimes against the Jews, which have been historically and legally acknowledged throughout the world. She's just the most recent one to make news.

Prominent Denier: David Irving

David Irving has been a thorn in the side of the judiciary, politicians and the media with his theories about the Second World War in general and the Holocaust in particular for a long time now. During the 1950s he was a steelworker in the Ruhr region, and learned to

"Holocaust deniers: Negating history," by Volker Wagener, Deutsche Welle, October 10, 2016. Reprinted by permission.

speak fluent German. He has written more than 30 non-fiction books about the National Socialist period. The British author came to prominence in 1963 with his book "The Destruction of Dresden" in which he cited fake documents to substantiate his claim that the number of victims was far higher than believed.

While at first Irving may have been regarded as an unconventional researcher, credited with referencing hitherto unknown sources, he has not been taken seriously as a historian since the late 1980s. That was when he first emerged as a Holocaust denier. Since then he has regularly aligned himself with right-wing extremists, principally in Germany.

The core message of his revisionist historical convictions is that Hitler neither ordered nor was aware of the extermination of the Jews. The Vienna district court sentenced Irving to three years imprisonment without probation for asserting that there were no concentration camps in Austria. He served two-thirds of his sentence, and has been refused entry to numerous countries ever since.

In 1993 the American historian Deborah Lipstadt described Irving as an "authentic Holocaust denier" who falsified facts and manipulated documents in his books. Irving sued her for libel, initiating his own financial ruin. In the year 2000 the High Court in London rejected his suit. Judge Charles Gray described Irving as "a right-wing pro-Nazi polemicist," stating that he was "an active Holocaust denier; that he was anti-Semitic and racist and that he associated with right-wing extremists who promoted neo-Nazism." Irving was ordered to pay the costs of the trial, totaling around 2.5 million pounds.

Prominent Denier: Bishop Richard Williamson

The theories of a high-ranking Catholic cleric have been causing a similar stir for years. The British bishop Richard Williamson denied the mass extermination of the Jews, and in doing so became the best-known representative of the Society of St. Pius X (SSPX). This renegade brotherhood of priests, founded in

1970 by the French Archbishop Marcel Lefebvre, devotes itself to fundamentalist Catholic tradition. It rejects the reforms of the Second Vatican Council (1962-1965), which, among other things, opened up the Catholic Church to ecumenical Christianity and the freedom of religion, and recognized Judaism as a path of salvation.

Williamson was already flatly denying the existence of gas chambers in 2008: "I believe that the historical evidence is hugely against six million Jews having been deliberately gassed in gas chambers as a deliberate policy of Adolf Hitler. I believe there were no gas chambers," he said. He also claimed that "the most serious conclude that between 200,000 and 300,000 Jews perished in Nazi concentration-camps. But not one of them by gassing in a gas-chamber."

These claims were made, on record, during an interview with a Swedish journalist. Knowing that Holocaust denial was a criminal offense in Germany punishable by up to five years in prison, Williamson asked for the interview to be published only in Sweden, and not online. The Swedish journalist ignored his request. The district court in Regensburg sentenced Williamson in absentia to 100 daily fines in lieu of jail time, at a rate of 100 euros per day. SSPX excommunicated Williamson in 2012 over a different matter.

Legal Consequences for Deniers

The punishment for Holocaust denial varies widely from one country to another. In the United States the right to freedom of speech also includes the right to dispute the extermination of the Jews. This is also the case in Great Britain, and this is why David Irving preferred to express himself in these countries.

However, Holocaust denial is now a criminal offense in several other European countries as well. Since 1992 Austria has been punishing those who "seek to deny, grossly trivialize, endorse or justify the National Socialist genocide or other National Socialist crimes against humanity." Two years prior to this, France also made it an offense punishable by law.

Historical denial is punishable in Belgium and Luxembourg, as well as in the Czech Republic and Poland, where the denial of Communist crimes is also an offence. In Spain, however, the law is different. In 2007 the Spanish constitutional court decided that its law against Holocaust denial infringed upon the right to freedom of expression.

Holocaust Denial Is Not Just Speech—It Poses a Threat to Society

Jeremy Bilfield

Jeremy Bilfield is currently employing statistical modeling in his work at the National Center for Juvenile Justice in Pittsburgh, Pennsylvania. He is a Jewish man who is passionate about utilizing the power of scientific thinking to illuminate the unknown and combat misinformation.

How do you begin to comprehend a denial of atrocity? How does one reconcile a genocide with, as scholar Deborah Lipstadt says, "the dubious distinction of being the best-documented genocide in the world" (TED & Lipstadt 2017) with the fact that there are individuals who discount every shred in the mountain of evidence? This is an understanding that I and every other Jewish individual must live with. Though we often feel that such beliefs are too crazy to be dangerous, I hope to help it be seen that these beliefs are far from innocuous.

We can define *Holocaust Denial* as an antisemitic belief that denies or manipulates, in part or whole, the reality of the Holocaust. (ADL 2019) Some common permutations of this include a rejection of the deaths of 6 million Jews at the hands of the Axis, a refutation of the method of any deaths which did occur, or assertions that the whole Holocaust is a hoax perpetuated by Jewish people to gain sympathy, money and the creation of Israel. (ADL 2019) All of these we can look into more deeply when we examine their evidence.

Yet "Deniers" come in many shapes and forms and may not always appear as you think. Surely, there are the usual suspects – skin-heads and those who explicitly call themselves Nazis or do not hide behind pretense (Southern Poverty Law Center 2017, Daily Stormer 2019). But they are also academics, politicians,

---

"Holocaust Denial: Extraordinary Belief, Extraordinarily Dangerous," by Jeremy Bilfield, The Ohio State University, February 28, 2019. Reprinted by permission.

neighbors (Austin 2019). As of January 2019, recently polling found that 1 in 20 Britons or 2,739,500 people do not believe the holocaust happened (Sherwood 2019). As recent as 2018, many individuals in Europe and the United States were unable to name even basic facts about the Holocaust—including 66% of millennials being unaware of what Auschwitz is (Gstalter 2018). Now, this is not to say that ignorance is tantamount to denial, but it certainly forms a fertile bed for those who would seek to lie to and reshape the uninformed.

This belief is extraordinary because it actively denies a plethora of accounts, stories, documents and other evidence both from the victims and the perpetrators (TED & Lipstadt 2017). It is a remarkably persistent belief, and it would not be surprising if its adherents are growing year by year right now. The Anti-Defamation League (an organization dedicated to combating antisemitism and racism) reported that antisemitic incidents grew by approximately 57% in 2017. (ADL 2018) Examples of public figures either directly supporting or tied to those who engage in Holocaust denial are present in both the left (Alice Walker, Jeremy Corbyn) and the right (Arthur Jones, Arthur King, David Icke, Benoît Loeuillet) in the US, UK, and France. (Grady 2018, Mendick 2017, Wilner 2018, Madhani 2018, Willsher 2017) Further and most alarmingly, a recent CNN survey of Europe found that 1/3 of Europeans believe that Jews use the Holocaust to advance their own position or goals. (CNN 2018, Dashefsky, Arnold, Ira 2017) Assuming this is representative, that's approximately 93.2 million people, a figure which gets only starker when you compare it to the total *World Jewish* population—only 14.5 million in 2017. (CNN 2018, Dashefsky, Arnold Ira 2017) Education may not be able to change the minds of those who have already written off this atrocity. But, for those not yet there, perhaps there is hope in spreading an understanding of the horror, and empathy for our still wounded communities.

Holocaust deniers use a variety of points to support their claims. Many of their points are a result of cherry-picked data or blatant falsehoods. In an effort to be "balanced," I will present the claim initially and respond to each as it is relevant. My list of denier "facts" is not exhaustive, for as a belief and form of antisemitism, it constantly shifts to include new "details" and "revisions."

First, deniers believe that the *Diary of Anne Frank* is a forgery. The diary was the result of Anne Frank, a young Jewish woman, recording her experiences as she hid with her family from the Nazis. Deniers say that due to the multiple editions of the diary or even its original form, it's fake. (Lipstadt 2011) Alternately, that the diary is written in green ballpoint pen, something that wouldn't be available to Anne easily at the time. (Lipstadt 2011) Both aspects of this are demonstrably false. Claims of the diary being fake were so numerous near its publication, that the Netherlands State Institute for War Documentation subjected the diary to many tests of its authenticity, showing that the handwriting, glue, paper, and ink of the diary were accurate both to the time period and to Anne herself. (Lipstadt 2011) Furthermore, that green writing was just on two pages, in the margins and never of the content itself. This brings into question whether the green writing was hers or an original editor but pulls it entirely away from the content. Finally, the reason for its multiple editions is due to Anne's own rewrites and attempts at writing a novel based on her experiences. (Lipstadt 2011)

Another belief is that the death figures in the Holocaust have been inflated. The proof here is supposed to be of the World Almanac which in 1940 listed the Jewish population at 15,319,359, then listed the population in 1949 as 15,713,638. (Pilcher 2007) The listed population growth, therefore, throws into question how many people died in the holocaust if any. But that number came instead not from the actually listed number for the World Almanac: 11,266,600, but from an error-filled 1950 report. (Pilcher 2007) Another source of "inflation" pointed to is the plaque change that occurred at the Auschwitz state museum in which the memorial plaque listed 1 million deaths in 1991 but before this listed 4 million deaths. Interestingly, this actually *was* inflation, but not by Jewish people, by the Soviets. The Soviets increased the number of non-jews who died in the camp, the number of Jewish individuals remains. (Pilcher 2007) Another popular counterpoint beneath this heading is that Jews didn't die, they simply fled to the USSR and US. This is oft touted by current tenured Northwestern University engineering professor Arthur Butz, who claims that the only reason Jews didn't re-establish contact with their relatives is bad marriages. (Lipstadt 2011) No evidence truly supports this claim, but we do have extensive records of those who did die. Such as the use of Nazi gas buses, chambers and the actual admittance of murder by the perpetrators (Lipstadt 2011).

As understanding of torture has shifted, some hold Nazi confessions were produced under torture and are false. Many deniers believe that there never was an intent to mass murder Jewish people. Confessions during the war crime trials were done under duress, they say. Why wouldn't someone confess to anything if it might save them from death? (Lipstadt 2011) Yet, many admissions of guilt were recorded after the sentencing of the Nazis, who therefore have no reason to lie. (Lipstadt 2011) Many explicitly claim the deaths of these Jews, such as Otto Ohlendorf, Einsatzgruppen commander who killed 90,000, or Adolf Eichmann, explicitly using the words *gassing the Jews*. (Lipstadt 2011)

Another belief is that documents of Auschwitz are false, as are other documents of death squads. Auschwitz often sits as the crown jewel in the minds of deniers. Deniers claim that many chambers in Auschwitz were used for delousing or that instead they were used for Air raids. They also supposed that the burning of dead bodies was a form of disease control. (Lipstadt 2011) Others claim that there were no gas chambers at all, a view espoused by Frenchmen Paul Rassiner, once imprisoned by the Nazis (Austin 2019, Memorial And Museum Auschwitz-Birkenau. 2019). Yet this ignored the many records of the death camp and many admissions by those that work there. (Lipstadt 2011) The gas chambers themselves have locks from the outside in and specifically made parts that refer to gas. Further, were the dead burned for disease control, the monthly burn rate of 120,000 bodies would have to be the result of 4/5 of the camp population dying of typhus in 1 month. That isn't possible in any epidemiological projection. (Lipstadt 2011) Finally, it again ignores the admissions of the killing method by Nazi Hans Stark, quoted by Deborah Lipstadt in her BBC article and again by me here:

"As early as autumn 1941 gassings were carried out in a room... [which] held 200 to 250 people, had a higher than average ceiling, no windows, only a specially insulated door with bolts like those of an airtight door [Luftschutzer]. The room had a flat roof, which allowed daylight in through the openings. It was through these openings that Zyklon B in granular form would be poured." (Lipstadt 2011)

When we accept that people do believe in these falsehoods when they actively or passively deny the Holocaust, the next logical question is why. Some extraordinary beliefs may come across as relatively harmless, but Holocaust Denial has a real effect on the survivors of the atrocity. I propose there are several cognitive contributions toward this belief, of which one might assign varying degrees of responsibility and malice to the individual.

First among them may be the *Just World Hypothesis*, which an idea that posits that people have a hard time believing such horrors may have actually occurred in the world. The death of 6 million Jews, a 1/3 of our total population, certainly qualifies for that. Perhaps these people have family members that lived in Germany or are German. These people are not bad people, how could such a thing happen? It is much easier to think that Jewish people simply ran away from the country, or that we weren't explicitly slated for extermination alongside Roma peoples. But the tattoos and records do not lie, they do not change.

Another possibility comes with the phenomenon of confirmation bias, in which one sees evidence and interprets it according to their own world view. In the libel trial of David Irving, (TED & Lipstadt 2017, Lipstadt 2011), the judge explicitly mentioned how the evidence provided by Irving were half-truths and misinformation. One may be able to look at a scattering of figures and pull out exactly what they want to see. Look – *the Auschwitz plaque changed, the death figures were inflated, there are multiple editions of Anne Frank's Journal!* All part truths interpreted just enough to support a denier. In cases where evidence may be cherry picked, one might instead point to a logically fallacy in reasoning—*The Texas Sharpshooter*. Drawing lines around just the areas that one might consider supportive to their point, manipulating data and numbers to their benefit.

It may also be possible the idea of a *True Believer* factors into Holocaust denial. The social context for these types of beliefs are important, and our recent polling shows that deniers may find themselves in good company, at all aspects and levels of society as previously described. Furthermore, when one comes out as a denier, it is nearly impossible to change, it is difficult to undo. Deniers then retreat to their own scientific journals, their own community to support themselves. Whenever they are challenged by the events of reality, the horrors suffered by Jewish people and others, they discount it. It's much easier to simply stay within their areas of belief.

Finally, and most insidiously, are those who are themselves racist by the application of stereotyping heuristics. In these cases, many deniers know that what they are doing is false. Lipstadt speaks much to this often as she did in her talk and in her trial with denier David Irving (TED & Lipstadt 2017, Lipstadt 2011). They attempt to spread their falsehoods to make Nazism more acceptable, a sentiment supported by the Nazis themselves (Pilcher 2007). These people believe that Jews are conniving, sneaky, that we are doing this to get our own state, to get money (Pilcher 2007). David Irving himself once asked a survivor how much money she received for the tattoo on her arm (TED & Lipstadt 2017). The loudest in this category are often the easiest to spot, but the quiet ones are just as bad. In the hearts of these people, they believe that Jews will always be this way—an enemy, an otherworldly evil to be exterminated.

To the horrors of the Holocaust, we Jewish people have coined the words "Never again.", but the truth of the matter is those outside of our group seem to be forgetting. Many Holocaust survivors are well past 80 years old, and a battery of psychological and cognitive faculties support the denial of our plight. People believe that a just world would never allow this, they think that their evidence supports them, and all else is a lie. Many have gone too far and now are *True Believers*, unable to turn back from what they have held before. Finally, more still ascribe to a racist heuristic, and will use Holocaust denial not out of belief, but as a weapon against Jews. In these cases, I write not for them, but for the others who have yet to be converted or are for some reason unsure. The only way that we can ensure this genocide does not repeat itself, is for the world to listen to us, hear us, and deny the deniers.

Works Cited

ADL. (2018). 2017 Audit of Anti-Semitic Incidents. Retrieved from https://www.adl.org/resources/reports/2017-audit-of-anti-semitic-incidents

ADL. (2019). Holocaust Denial. Retrieved from https://www.adl.org/resources/glossary-terms/holocaust-denial

Austin, B. S. (2019). Holocaust Denial: A Brief History. Retrieved from https://www.jewishvirtuallibrary.org/a-brief-history-of-holocaust-denial

CNN. (2018). A Shadow Over Europe. Retrieved from https://edition.cnn.com/interactive/2018/11/europe/antisemitism-poll-2018-intl/

DailyStormer. (2019). Tag Archives: Holocaust. Retrieved from https://dailystormer.name/tag/holocaust/

Dashefsky, Arnold/Sheskin, & Ira. (2017). Vital Statistics. Retrieved from https://www.jewishvirtuallibrary.org/jewish-population-of-the-world

Grady, C. (2018, December 20). The Alice Walker anti-Semitism controversy, explained. Retrieved from https://www.vox.com/culture/2018/12/20/18146628/alice-walker-david-icke-anti-semitic-new-york-times

Gstalter, M. (2018, April 12). Poll: Majority of Americans say something like the Holocaust could happen again. Retrieved from https://thehill.com/blogs/blog-briefing-room/news/382843-poll-majority-of-americans-say-something-like-the-holocaust

Lipstadt, D. (2011, February 17). History – World Wars: Denying the Holocaust. Retrieved from http://www.bbc.co.uk/history/worldwars/genocide/deniers_01.shtml

Madhani, A. (2018, November 07). 56,000 voters in Illinois House district preferred Holocaust denier to moderate Democrat. Retrieved from https://www.usatoday.com/story/news/politics/elections/2018/11/07/holocaust-denier-neo-nazi-arthur-jones-chicago-illinois-dan-lipinski/1918933002/

Memorial And Museum Auschwitz-Birkenau. (2019). Auschwitz-Birkenau. Retrieved from http://auschwitz.org/en/history/holocaust-denial/denial-forms/

Mendick, R. (2017, May 20). Jeremy Corbyn's 10-year association with group which denies the Holocaust. Retrieved from https://www.telegraph.co.uk/news/2017/05/20/jeremy-corbyns-10-year-association-group-denies-holocaust/

Pilcher, B. R. (2007, November 19). Holocaust Denial. Retrieved from https://www.myjewishlearning.com/article/holocaust-denial/

Sherwood, H. (2019, January 27). One in 20 Britons 'does not believe' Holocaust took place, poll finds. Retrieved from https://www.theguardian.com/world/2019/jan/27/one-in-20-britons-does-not-believe-holocaust-happened

Southern Poverty Law Center. (2017). Holocaust Denial. Retrieved from https://www.splcenter.org/fighting-hate/extremist-files/ideology/holocaust-denial

TED, & Lipstadt, D. (2017, May 23). Behind the lies of Holocaust denial | Deborah Lipstadt. Retrieved from https://www.youtube.com/watch?v=0ztdofPc8Rw

Willsher, K. (2017, March 15). France's Front National suspends party official over Holocaust denial. Retrieved from https://www.theguardian.com/world/2017/mar/15/benoit-loeuillet-france-front-national-holocaust-denial

Wilner, M. (2018, October 27). U.S. Rep. King after Auschwitz visit: "Bring pride back to Germany again". Retrieved from https://www.jpost.com/Diaspora/US-Rep-King-after-Auschwitz-visit-Bring-pride-back-to-Germany-again-570398

Holocaust Denial Is Hate Speech That Should Not Be Defended

Elana Heideman

Elana Heideman is a Holocaust scholar who serves as the Executive Director of the Israel Forever Foundation. Her expertise is in psychology, identity development, and empowerment training. Heideman earned her PhD under Nobel Prize recipient and Holocaust survivor Professor Elie Wiesel.

Facebook is one of the most influential companies in our time. Its existence has changed social interactions and the way information is disseminated throughout society and across the globe.

Recently the issue of free speech vs censorship on Facebook has come into the limelight due to the statements of the company's founder and CEO declaring that Holocaust deniers will not be removed or censored.

The company is known for their "mission to desire to make the world more open and connected….To facilitate this goal, we also work hard to make our platform a safe and respectful place for sharing and connection." As part of the implementation of this mission Facebook has published a very detailed explanation of their community standards, including types of speech that are not allowed on their platform:

> We do not allow hate speech on Facebook because it creates an environment of intimidation and exclusion and in some cases may promote real-world violence. We define hate speech as a direct attack on people based on what we call protected characteristics — race, ethnicity, national origin, religious affiliation, sexual orientation, sex, gender, gender identity, and serious disability or disease. We also provide some protections for immigration status. We define attack as violent

"Denying The 'Right' To Holocaust Denial," Dr. Elana Heideman, The Israel Forever Foundation. Reprinted by permission.

or dehumanizing speech, statements of inferiority, or calls for exclusion or segregation.

We are left to wonder, how is it possible to not view the denial of the Holocaust, the attempt to exterminate the Jewish People, the Nation of Israel, based on nothing but their religious and enthno-tribal affiliation, as hate speech? Furthermore, when it is known that incitement against Jews and Israelis in particular has led to terrorists murdering Jews, how can Facebook let this most basic of incitements stand?

If nothing else, what about the company's statements about: *"Reducing the spread of false news on Facebook is a responsibility that we take seriously. We also recognize that this is a challenging and sensitive issue. We want to help people stay informed without stifling productive public discourse"*?

Five Facts About This Story You Need to Know

1. Zuckerberg said Facebook would not take down hate speech denying the Holocaust because it 'prioritizes allowing people to express themselves, even if they get things wrong'
2. Facebook has been promoting Holocaust denial groups at the top of its search results. No other major search engines promote Holocaust denialism in their search results when users search for "Holocaust."
3. When contacted about promoting Holocaust denial groups at the top of search results, Facebook said it made a mistake and had "corrected the issue."
4. Germany issued a critique of the recent announcement, stating that such a policy was contrary to German law. "There must be no place for anti-Semitism. This includes verbal and physical attacks on Jews as well as the denial of the Holocaust," Justice Minister Katarina Barley said. "The latter is also punishable by us and will be strictly prosecuted."

5. Anti-Defamation League CEO Jonathan Greenblatt challenged Zuckerberg, saying that Holocaust denial is "a willful, deliberate and longstanding deception tactic by anti-Semites that is incontrovertibly hateful, hurtful, and threatening to Jews. Facebook has a moral and ethical obligation not to allow its dissemination."

We believe that this is unacceptable. Israel Forever's interns, young as they are, offer a voice of clear moral reason. There is no "right" to deny the Holocaust.

ELLIOT: If Facebook is going to combat other hatred, they have to combat anti-semitic posts as well. Otherwise let there be freedom of speech for all hatred.

ERIC: With so much ignorance in the world, it's important to separate fact from fiction.

- Fact: the Holocaust happened.
- Fact: 6 million Jews perished in the Holocaust
- Fact: Denying the Holocaust is a denial of historic reality

Allowing for Holocaust deniers to have an uninhibited voice on Facebook only serves to foster ignorance and Antisemitism. Facebook is not the platform to spread fiction.

JORDAN: I don't agree with the measures that Mark Zuckerberg, a Jew himself, has taken to address the Holocaust deniers free speech on Facebook. This is a mainstream social media platform, used by millions of people across the world, where an allowance of open and real Antisemitic acts are occurring and not immediately being taken down. Because of its power, Facebook should hold values to ensure that all of their users feel safe and are not blatantly targeted.

Denial of The Holocaust is a threat to the Jewish people. It is the recognition of hate towards the Jewish people. The fact that Facebook allows this to continue, allows for continued hate. Zuckerberg should be ashamed to be ok with denial of his ancestral blood. As the leader of Facebook with their own morals, as well as his own morals raising children Jewish, how is the Jewish population supposed to respond? Now we are normalizing the denial of the Holocaust and promoting people to continue to believe something that is false but think it's real because they "saw it on Facebook"? It's not fair and it's frankly cowardly.

I wholeheartedly believe people make mistakes, and deserve freedom of speech but I do not condone hate speech. Whether against Jews or not, it's not ok, and it's not humane. However, it is also fact that Facebook does not allow hate speech against other ethnicities, but it is apparent that there is hate against Jews and there is nothing being done about it. So fix it.

HARLEY: Instead of Facebook allowing Holocaust deniers to continue spreading their false claims in order to promote freedom of speech, it should be educating their wrongly informed users on the traumatic historical event that will forever affect the Jewish community.

RACHEL: There has to be a line drawn between free speech and the defamation of a group of people, by allowing the Holocaust deniers to exist on Facebook, Zuckerberg is allowing for the continued efforts to tear down the Jewish people. Why is that a Rabbi loses access to his facebook page for a study abroad program in Israel but posts denying the Holocaust are able to stand running? This is not a free speech issue as he says, it is simply allowing Antisemitism to continue to rise despite Zuckerberg being a Jew himself. Time and time again Jews are being censored for our views, how come Judaism and pro Israel statements are not considered acceptable free speech? Why is it free speech when it is against the Jews but not for the Jews?

ABBY: As our world is supposedly moving towards a more "accepting" and "diverse" society, it seems to be that Jews are continuously excluded from these movements and mindsets. "We must accept everyone and make all people feel welcome in their country of origin!" Except the Jews.

Facebook, which was created to be a social platform and a way for people across the world to connect, is being used as a tactic for blatant Antisemitism. Holocaust denial is not free speech. It is hate speech. It is complete and utter hatred against Jewish people because it is aimed at denying the murder of 6 million Jews, but not denying the murder of the hundreds of thousands of disabled people, homosexuals, gypsies, blacks and political dissidents.

As a Jewish person, I would no longer want to be a part of the Facebook community. It is supposed to be a safe place for people to express themselves and their views, but apparently this is not the case if you are Jewish.

Mark Zuckerberg, you should be ashamed of yourself. You are aiding and abetting to the rise of Antisemitism across the world and you are hurting your own people. What happens when your Jewish children grow up and they see that their father encouraged people, on his established platform, to deny and allow denial of the genocide of their ancestors?

Here's my message to you, Zuckerberg. You will not break us. Your allowance of Holocaust denial talk on your platform will not take away from the fact that the Holocaust DID happen and over 6 million Jews WERE murdered. I, as a proud Jew, will always stand up to bullies like you and I will never let you diminish my pride. The people of Israel are alive and you cannot and will not change this.

LEORA: There is no room in society for Holocaust denial. And the leaders of the social network have the duty to make sure of that. Free speech, for example, attests to one's views of the international response to The Holocaust, or the expression of solidarity with either party. Free speech does not entail denying the Holocaust. Denying the systematic torture and murder of the Jewish Nation must be recognized for what it is, hate speech. It is responsible of those managing the social network, with all its influence and innovation, to be cautious of its rules and restrictions.

But they must not mix-up categories, because that has its own dire consequences. Free speech and hate speech are distinct. Learning about the Holocaust, understanding what happened, is important not only in Jewish history but in the history of mankind. Thus, the creators of the social network have a greater duty to humanity and so a duty to expel those who deprive us of the ability to learn from past faults and to ultimately strive for good.

MARSHALL: After seeing the first news articles and tweets that Zuckerberg was defending Holocaust deniers, I couldn't believe my eyes. I kept thinking on how the media must have twisted his words or how he misspoke in an interview. But contrary to my belief everything I was reading was true. Mark Zuckerberg, a Jew himself was standing up for deniers and providing them a platform.

I found that after the 2015 Paris attacks Mark Zuckerberg said in a statement "As a Jew, my parents taught me that we must stand up against attacks on all communities. Even if an attack isn't against you today, in time attacks on freedom for anyone will hurt everyone." Ironically I believe he doesn't apply this thinking to his own community, who raised him to become the successful entrepreneur that he is today. If he truly believed this he wouldn't allow Holocaust deniers to spread the misinformation that they are on Facebook. Allowing them to do so is allowing an attack on every Jew around the world (not to mention an insult to the six million Jews who were murdered in the Holocaust!).

As Zuckerberg looked back on the way Facebook handled fake news in the past election cycle he said "calling that crazy was dismissive and I regret it," one thing is for sure in the future Zuckerberg will realize how naive he was by allowing Holocaust deniers a platform.

I do not agree with Zuckbergs approach to this, as we say "Never Forget" about the Holocaust we must also say that we will never let people spread false tales to minimize the atrocity that occurred on our people.

Another perspective: As I asked my roommates their opinions, one of them said its freedom of speech and by allowing them to use facebook as a platform it will enable us to find them and discredit them. But what happens when they are not discredited? What happens when these outrageous and sickening statements are allowed to stand and actually believed by those who don't take the time to learn the truth?

ONDRIA: Everyone knows there is a fine line between what constitutes as freedom of speech and what is a hate crime. It is one thing for an individual to have hateful opinions, but it is quite another to use social media to spread anti-Semitism and other hate in order to create a norm against the targeted victim group.

Facebook was not meant to be a news outlet; it is not meant to be taken seriously, but in the era of "fake news," people take advantage that their opinions can become so widespread without any knowledge on a subject and that misinformation is passed on to others who are unfamiliar with the subject. The fact that Mark Zuckerberg is a Jew himself and allowing such disgusting lies go viral about the Holocaust and stand up for those who incite violence against Jews is pathetic.

SOPHIE: Holocaust denial is hate speech. It is an attack on the Jewish people. It is an attack on truth. Holocaust denial de-legitimizes history and the plight of the Jewish people thus having anti-semitism intentions. As a Jew himself, Zuckerberg should be aware of the dangerous implications of these convoluted intentions and the serious damage they can cause for a nation of people.

AUBRIE: Holocaust denial is dangerous. As time goes on and we get further away from the horrific event that was the Holocaust more and more people are not knowledgeable about it's occurrence or the events that took place. If we allow the memory of the Holocaust to fade and allow Holocaust deniers to prevail it will only cast a darker shadow in people's memory of the Holocaust and will soon be forgotten or be believed that it never happened.

The Limits of Free Speech in the Classroom and Beyond

Jennifer Rich

Jennifer Rich is an assistant professor in the department of sociology and anthropology at Rowan University in New Jersey, where she is also director of the Rowan Center for Holocaust and Genocide Studies.

When I first set out to research how the Holocaust was being depicted in textbooks in New Jersey's public schools, my hope was to see what students were being taught about the systematic state-sponsored killing of 6 million Jewish men, women and and children.

I never imagined that my work would lead me to serve as a witness against a history teacher who encouraged his students to question whether the Holocaust had ever taken place at all.

The case—known as Jason Mostafa Ali v. Woodbridge Township School District—represents a rare look inside the mind of what I see as a modern day Holocaust denier. In some ways, the case is reminiscent of Irving v. Penguin and Lipstadt—a Holocaust denial case famously portrayed in the 2016 movie "Denial" and written about in a book of the same name.

In that case, Emory University history professor Deborah Lipstadt was sued for libel in a London court by author David Irving, a well-known writer about WWII. Irving filed the libel suit after Lipstadt wrote a book called "Denying the Holocaust," in which she called Irving "one of the most dangerous spokespersons for Holocaust denial." A British court ultimately tossed out Irving's suit, finding that he had "persistently and deliberately misrepresented and manipulated historical evidence" in order to portray Hitler in "unwarrantedly favourable light."

"I was an expert witness against a teacher who taught students to question the Holocaust," by Jennifer Rich, The Conversation, May 30, 2019, https://theconversation.com/i-was-an-expert-witness-against-a-teacher-who-taught-students-to-question-the-holocaust-116578. Licensed under CC BY-ND 4.0 International.

Now here I was some two decades later, being called upon to serve as a witness against a schoolteacher trying to get his job back after being fired for doing essentially the same thing.

My grandparents were Holocaust survivors. I have also spent the past four years interviewing children and other grandchildren of Holocaust survivors. My work shows how deeply members of the second and third generations feel the impact of the Holocaust in their lives. Many often feel like they carry the trauma that parents and grandparents experienced. I had to work to keep my emotions in check and focus on the business at hand.

Denial Makes News

My involvement in the case against Mr. Ali began in November 2017 when I got a phone call from a lawyer who was representing the Woodbridge Township School District. I had sent an email earlier in the year to the district about my study of how textbooks portray the Holocaust and officials there remembered my note.

Woodbridge officials had fired Mr. Ali, who was teaching students to question the Holocaust and who was also pushing 9/11 conspiracy theories. Mr. Ali was now suing the district for illegally firing him over his race and religion.

Mr. Ali had first made headlines in September 2016 after a news station discovered several 9/11 conspiracy links on his school webpage.

After speaking with the Woodbridge district lawyer, I was sent several hundred pages of depositions, student work and lesson plans to review. I was also asked if I would serve as an expert witness in the case.

One particularly memorable student paper in the documents was called "A Gas Chamber Full of Lies."

"We have all been taught that the Holocaust was a time of hate, and that Hitler used the gifts he possessed for absolute evil, but is that really the case? ... Is the death of the Jews completely justified? No, because nobody deserves to die, regardless what they've done. But are their deaths really completely unjustified either?" read an excerpt.

Another student stated that the Jews imprisoned in concentration camps "had a much easier and more enjoyable life in the camps" and that "even though they were not at home, they felt like they were."

Mr. Ali's pedagogical folly was not limited to the Holocaust. He also shared links to stories that asserted that 9/11 was a conspiracy between the CIA and Mossad. The stories had headlines like "The Jews are like a cancer, woe to the world if they become strong."

Confronted with this evidence, I decided to serve as an expert witness in the case.

Taking On a 'Content Specialist'

In a report to the court, I pointed out how—during a deposition—Mr. Ali made numerous factual errors and had a lack of knowledge about the Second World War and the Holocaust.

Mr. Ali did not know basic facts, such as the name of General Erwin Rommel, one of the most prominent German generals of the war. He also was ignorant of Elie Wiesel or Wiesel's classic book "Night," perhaps the best-known account of the Holocaust by an Auschwitz survivor.

These giant gaps in basic factual knowledge, I told the court, came along with what I described as a "worrisome awareness of arcane, conspiracy-related details, a classic case of losing the forest for the trees in historical terms."

"By allowing his students to investigate assertions, myths, and logical fallacies as if they are real, Mr. Ali created the space for denial to grow," I wrote in my report. "This allows the idea of 'maybe there is more to this than I was told' to bloom."

Where Free Speech Stops

In Mr. Ali's case, he alleged—among other things—that he had a First Amendment right to share materials that he saw fit.

When he was asked whether he taught his students to "question the facts as to whether Hitler chose to brutally abuse, take advantage, starve and murder Jews for absolutely no reason at all," Mr. Ali responded that he taught his students to "question everything." And when he was asked if he encouraged his students to "come to different views than the traditional understanding of what World War II and the Holocaust and Hitler were about," he stated: "Yeah, it's called debate."

But United States District Judge Madeline Cox Arleo disagreed. She ruled that the school district, not the classroom teacher, "has the ultimate right to decide what will be taught in the classroom." Except for a procedural matter unrelated to his teaching, she tossed out the various claims in Mr. Ali's lawsuit, saying that he failed to show he was fired for anything other than the reasons given by the school district—not his race or his religion like he claimed.

Mr. Ali is not done with this fight. Even though a judge tossed out his lawsuit, on May 28 he filed an appeal, court records show.

The Conversation reached out to Mr. Ali and his attorney, Nicholas Pompelio, but did not get a response.

I don't doubt that Mr. Ali has a story to tell. I can't speak to his claims that he was subjected to an "anti-Muslim attitude" at work, or that the school district didn't seem to have a problem with his 9/11 conspiracy theory lessons until a TV station started reporting about it.

All I know is that when it comes to what Mr. Ali either let or encouraged his students to believe when it comes to Hitler and the Holocaust, his lessons weren't just wrong, they were dangerous.

CHAPTER 4

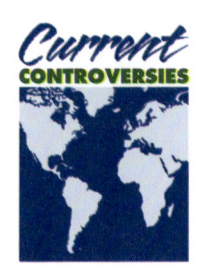

Can Conspiracy Theories Be Stopped?

Many Factors Are at Play in Conspiracy Theorizing

Kendra Cherry

Kendra Cherry is an author and educator who has written for publications like the New York Times *and* Psychology Today.

There has been a growing interest in recent years in why people believe in conspiracy theories. Recent controversial examples of such theories include the belief that terrorist attacks and mass shootings were staged events orchestrated by the U.S. government. Other examples include the belief that the pharmaceutical industry intentionally spreads diseases or that vaccines cause illness rather than prevent them.

While it might seem like these beliefs are rare or even pathological, research has shown that they are surprisingly common. Polls suggest that over one-third of U.S. adults believe that global warming is a hoax. Another study found that half of all Americans believe in at least one conspiracy theory.

What explains this common and often deep-rooted belief that powerful, sinister, and secretive groups are conspiring to deceive others—particularly in a day and age where we have more access to information and facts that might debunk many of these ideas? Researchers suspect that there are a number of psychological mechanisms that contribute to these beliefs, many of which may be the result of evolutionary processes.

In a world where you might feel powerless and alienated, it can be appealing to believe that there are forces plotting against your interests. Once these beliefs take root, cognitive biases and mental shortcuts reinforce and strengthen them. Many of the same factors that fuel other types of problematic thinking, such as a belief in the paranormal, also contribute to conspiracy theories. And while

"Why People Believe in Conspiracy Theories," by Kendra Cherry, Verywell Mind, Dotdash Publishing Family, June 17, 2019. Reprinted by permission.

such paranoid ideas are not new, the internet has helped transform the way and the speed in which they are spread.

In order to understand why people believe in these conspiracies, it is important to explore some of the psychological explanations and the potential effects these beliefs have.

What Is a Conspiracy Theory?

A conspiracy theory can be defined as the belief that there are groups that meet in secret to plan and carry out malevolent goals.

Explanations

Researchers suggest that there are a number of different reasons why people believe in conspiracy theories. Many of these explanations boil down to three key driving factors:

- A need for understanding and consistency (epistemic)
- A need for control (existential)
- A need to belong or feel special (social)

Epistemic Reasons

Epistemic explanations refer to the desire to derive certainty and understanding. The world can be a confusing place filled with events that may seem dangerous and chaotic. People are driven to explain the things that happen in the world around them. Doing so helps them build up a consistent, stable, and clear understanding of how the world works.

When people encounter disparate information, it is only natural to look for explanations that connect the dots. Conspiracy theories offer explanations that provide this connection. They also suggest that the underlying causes are hidden from public view. When confusing things happen, believers can then assume that it is because they are being intentionally deceived by outside forces.

There is also a connection between conspiracy beliefs and educational levels. Lower educational status tends to be associated with higher levels of conspiracy belief.

Having lower analytical abilities and less tolerance for uncertainty also play a role. As a result, people turn to conspiracy theories to provide explanations for events that seem confusing or frightening.

The confirmation bias can also play a role in the development of conspiracy belief. People are naturally inclined to seek out information that confirms their existing beliefs. So when they run across a theory that supports something that they already think is true, they are more likely to believe the information is also true.

Factors That Increase Conspiracy Belief

- In situations involving large-scale events, where more mundane or small-scale explanations seem inadequate
- In situations where people experience distress over uncertainty

Existential Reasons

There is also evidence that people turn to conspiracy theories as a way of feeling safer and more in control. When people feel threatened in some way, detecting sources of danger can be a way of coping with anxiety.

While researchers understand these existential motivations, there is little evidence that believing in these theories actually helps people satisfy their need to feel control and autonomy. In fact, by believing in these theories, people may actually be less likely to engage in actions that would potentially boost their sense of control (such as voting or participating in political activity).

So while people may be drawn to conspiracy theories as a way of making sense of the world and feeling more in control of their own destiny, the long-term effects may actually leave people feeling more disempowered than ever before.

What the Research Suggests

- One study found that people who feel psychologically and sociopolitically disempowered are more likely to believe in conspiracy theories.
- Another study found that people are also more likely to believe in conspiracies when they are experiencing anxiety.

Social Reasons

People can also be motivated to believe in conspiracy due to social reasons. Some researchers have hypothesized that by believing in conspiracies that cast out-groups as the opposition, people are able to feel better about themselves and their own social group. Those who believe in the conspiracy feel that they are the "heroes" of the story, while those who are conspiring against them are "the enemy."

Such findings suggest that conspiracy belief might arise as a sort of defense mechanism. When people feel disadvantaged, they are motivated to find ways to boost their own self-perceptions. Blaming others by linking them to malevolent plots provides a scapegoat on which to lay blame, thus improving how conspiracy believers view themselves.

The belief in conspiracies is also rooted in what is referred to as collective narcissism. This is the belief that your own social group is better, yet less appreciated, by other people.

People who feel that they or their social group have been victimized are also less likely to believe in government institutions and more likely to believe in conspiracies.

The way in which people encounter and share these ideas should also be noted. It's easy to dismiss a story shared by a random source that you don't trust. But when multiple people in your social circle who you *do* know and trust all seem to believe the same story, it starts to seem less like a silly conspiracy and more like a trusted fact. Sharing these kinds of stories within our networks gives social credence to such conspiratorial thinking.

People Believe in Conspiracy Theories When:

- They are on the "losing" side of a political issue
- They have a lower social status due to income or ethnicity
- They have experienced social ostracism
- They are prejudiced against "enemy" groups they perceive as powerful

Effects

While researchers have some good theories about why people believe in conspiracies, it is less clear what the ultimate effects of these beliefs are.

What researchers have found is that while these beliefs are motivated by a desire to understand, exert control, and feel socially connected, these aren't the effects people are deriving from their beliefs. Rather than fulfilling these needs, believing in conspiracies seems to reinforce feelings of confusion, isolation, disenfranchisement, and loneliness. It is a destructive cycle - negative feelings contribute to the belief in conspiracies, yet the belief in conspiracies results in negative feelings.

Believing in conspiracy theories erodes people's trust in their government, their leaders, and their institutions. It also diminishes trust in science and research itself. This distrust may discourage people from participating in their social worlds. It might also cause people to stop seeing themselves as valuable contributors to society.

Rather than helping people cope with their feelings of social alienation and political disenfranchisement, conspiracy beliefs seem to create a cycle of distrust that leads to even greater disempowerment.

Risks

Believing in things that are not true poses a number of dangers, which can have real effects that impact individual behavior and ultimately have a ripple impact on society as a whole. A resurgence in Measles outbreaks in the U.S. has been largely attributed to a refusal by some individuals to vaccinate—a refusal that stems largely from the conspiratorial belief that vaccines cause autism and other health ailments.

Failing to address dangerous misbeliefs presents a potential danger to public health and even the political process itself. Faulty beliefs lead can lead people to not vaccinate, not vote, or, in some rare cases, even engage in dangerous or violent behavior.

Overcoming Conspiracy Theory Beliefs

In the age of disinformation, finding ways to refute conspiracy beliefs seems more important than ever. Social platforms claim to be buckling down on those who peddle and profit off of conspiracies, but is it really possible to change such views once they've taken root?

One problem faced when trying to disprove conspiracy theories is that people who hold these beliefs also tend to suspect that there are factions engaged in covering up these activities. Those trying to debunk the mistaken beliefs are then viewed as simply being actors in the conspiracy itself.

While it might be tempting to simply mock conspiracy theories, especially the more ridiculous ones, this usually causes believers to dig in their heels and deepen their commitment to their belief.

Many factors that contribute to conspiratorial beliefs, such as educational background and personality, are not easily or quickly changed. Researchers have found one tactic, however, that is effective—encouraging believers to pursue their goals.

People tend to take one of two approaches in the pursuit of goals.

- Those who are "promotion-focused" believe that they have the power and control to shape their future.
- People who are "prevention-focused," on the other hand, are more focused on protecting what they already have rather than on achieving their goals.

Feeling In Control Reduces Conspiratorial Thinking

So what does this have to do with conspiracy beliefs? Researchers found that promotion-focused people were more skeptical and less likely to buy into conspiracies. Why? People who believe that the future hinges on their own actions have a great deal of personal agency and control. It is this sense of autonomy and agency that makes people less likely to believe in secret plots and nefarious plans.

What the researchers also discovered was that giving people a nudge in the direction of a more promotion-focused mindset could actually reduce belief in conspiracies. In practical terms, promoting messages that help people feel more in control can minimize conspiratorial thinking.

While researchers have been able to reduce conspiratorial thinking in the lab, how applicable is this in the real world? In workplace settings, managers might employ this strategy to help minimize water-cooler worries, office gossip, and interpersonal friction. Regular discussions that center on employee goals and strategies to achieve those goals can help keep workers feeling more in control and less subject to corporate whims.

In terms of public health, organizations might start by promoting messages focused on realistic things people can do to take control of their own health. Building this sort of action-oriented mindset may help discourage belief in health-related conspiracies and build greater trust between medical organizations and health consumers.

Write It Down
Researchers had study participants write down their aspirations, which helped them focus on their goals and what they could do to achieve them. This simple activity encourages people to take a more promotion-focused mindset and reduces conspiracy belief.

A Word from Verywell
Conspiratorial thinking can be problematic and dangerous (Pizzagate, anyone?), but this does not mean that skepticism of institutions, marketing, and media messaging is not warranted. After all, not all conspiracies are false (the Tuskegee experiments and Iran-Contra are just a couple of examples).

As you encounter information from various sources, it is important to be able to distinguish between false conspiracy theories and real threats to personal security. While it may be tempting to ridicule conspiracy believers, remember that these sort of beliefs are actually pretty common—you probably even believe in some of them. In a world where people feel the very real effects of power imbalances and distrust in leadership, conspiracy theories will naturally flourish, which means discouraging this type of thinking is not always easy.

It Is Difficult, but Possible, to Counter Conspiracy Theories in Court

Enrique Armijo

Enrique Armijo is associate dean for academic affairs and an associate professor at Elon University School of Law in North Carolina.

Alex Jones, a well-known media personality, falsely claims you were an accomplice in faking the murder of your own child. You sue him.

It seems such a case should be easy to win, given the nature of those statements. But defamation law does not provide an equally easy answer.

I am a legal scholar who studies the intersection between the First Amendment and online speech. A court battle now being fought illustrates the difficulties in winning such a case, and how current law needs modernizing in order to address the needs of the aggrieved and the ways we talk about public tragedies.

Sandy Hook: Fact and Fiction

Here's the background: On Dec. 14, 2012, gunman Adam Lanza shot and killed 20 6- and 7-year-olds at the Sandy Hook Elementary School in Newtown, Connecticut.

For several years afterward, Infowars host and conspiracy theorist Alex Jones questioned whether the shooting was faked by the Obama White House and co-conspirators in an effort to undermine gun rights in the United States.

Among other statements, Jones claimed that the shooting was a "giant hoax," was "staged" and had "inside job written all over it." He claimed that traumatized families and students were "lying ... actors" in front of a CNN blue screen during Anderson

---

"Falsehoods, Sandy Hook and suing Alex Jones," by Enrique Armijo, The Conversation, June 1, 2018. https://theconversation.com/falsehoods-sandy-hook-and-suing-alex-jones-97056. Licensed under CC BY-ND 4.0 International.

Cooper's reporting from Connecticut. Jones compared the scene at the school to a Disney World hologram.

Sandy Hook parents were also harassed online and in person as "hoaxers" and "crisis actors" by members of Jones' audience.

In 2017, a reporter on Jones's show claimed that one of the Sandy Hook parents was lying when he said he held his son and saw a bullet hole in his son's head, since the slain students were identified via photographs. In fact, the coroner released the victims' bodies to their families for funeral purposes, so the parent's claim was true.

So this spring, several of the parents of children who died in the shooting at Sandy Hook sued Jones for defamation.

Narrow Standards for Defamation

For hundreds of years, the parents' defamation claim would have been a simple one decided under state law. Jones' false allegations that the parents lied would have been deemed harmful to the parents' reputations; a jury would assume money damages were appropriate; and Jones would have had to pay.

However, that changed in 1964 when the U.S. Supreme Court, in New York Times v. Sullivan, decided that the federal Constitution's First Amendment required state courts to strike a different balance.

Post-Sullivan, the First Amendment, which generally protects speakers from government interference, now had a significant role to play in defamation law, which has long given individuals the right to sue based on oral and written statements that harmed their reputation.

In Sullivan, the court decided that where the plaintiff claiming she was defamed by a defendant's statement was a "public official"—a politician or other high-level government officer—state defamation law had to be more lenient in order to protect the public's right to vigorously discuss such people, even where statements in that discussion turn out to be false.

The court carved out this leeway by changing the standard of proof that the public official plaintiff had to show as part of her defamation claim.

Instead of simply showing that the defamatory statement was false, or showing that a reasonable speaker would have known the statement was false—which is the standard that still applies to private people in many states—the plaintiff had to show that the defendant either deliberately lied about her or seriously doubted the statement was true and said it anyway.

That standard is known as "actual malice."

In other words, by protecting individuals' rights to speak freely about people in power, the court promoted the democratic process at the expense of possible harms to the reputations of public officials.

Ten years later, in Gertz v. Welch, the court extended the actual malice standard to a new class of defamation plaintiffs. The court called them "limited-purpose public figures" – otherwise private people who had voluntarily inserted themselves into controversies that were the subject of public discussion.

These people, concluded the court, should, like public officials, also have to show actual malice in defamation suits. That's because they assume the risk, the court said, of being talked about negatively and even falsely when they enter public debates "in order to influence the resolution of the issues involved."

But what if a person didn't choose to be a public figure? Should they still be treated as one when they sued a speaker for defamation?

The court said that "hypothetically, it may be possible for someone to become a public figure through no purposeful action of his own, but the instances of truly involuntary public figures must be exceedingly rare."

Count the families of the Sandy Hook dead among those rare involuntary public figures.

Technology Complicates Defamation

As I've written before, the internet has changed defamation law in deep and meaningful ways.

It has allowed prospective defamation plaintiffs to defend their reputations without resorting to lawsuits, by responding to stories about them online. Conversely, it has also helped authors correct disputed or false facts about story subjects more quickly and easily.

But the internet has also undermined the court's statement in Gertz that the problem of an involuntary limited-purpose public figure was unlikely to occur.

By making public so much of daily life that was formerly private, the internet has made involuntary public figures out of many people who have suffered notable tragedies through no fault or risky behavior of their own.

All of which brings us back to Alex Jones.

In his legal defense, Jones will likely argue that the plaintiff-parents are limited-purpose public figures—that they have inserted themselves into the larger controversy around gun rights in the U.S.—and they should therefore have to prove that his statements about them were made with knowledge that they were false.

True, many Sandy Hook parents became vocal participants in the anti-gun movement in the wake of the tragedy. Several have sued the maker of the gun used in the shooting. Others have organized online to try and prevent future similar attacks, and gone online to call for greater gun control.

But making such individuals prove actual malice in their defamation suit against Jones—a much tougher standard to prove—would get the First Amendment backwards. It would stifle important responses to disastrous events in individuals' private lives.

It would encourage individuals to take the tragedies that happen to them and swallow them silently.

No one would have volunteered for the kind of attention that the Sandy Hook parents have received. But if a court were to find that they were public figures because of that attention, then future parents might not speak out at all, which would do significant harm to the marketplace of ideas that the First Amendment is intended to promote.

Parents have the right to decide whether to grieve their children publicly or privately, and online or off. The degree of fault they might have to show in a defamation claim should not play any role in that decision.

Education Could Be a Path to Reducing Widespread Belief in Conspiracy Theories

Tania Lombrozo

Tania Lombrozo is a professor of psychology at Princeton University.

Debunked conspiracy theories have been making the rounds on social media lately, from the thoroughly unsupported claim that millions of people voted illegally in California to false assertions about paid protesters being bused to demonstrations.

Conspiracy theories, which typically involve one or more powerful agents secretly manipulating world events, are accepted by a large proportion of Americans. One analysis of four nationally representative surveys found that half of respondents endorsed at least one conspiracy theory, such as the claim that Barack Obama was born outside the United States or that the financial crisis was deliberately orchestrated by a group of Wall Street bankers.

Because conspiracy theories can influence people's attitudes towards individuals, social groups, institutions and policies, they're often of interest to those tracking public opinion and individual behavior.

But they're also of interest to psychologists for what they reveal about the human mind. What makes conspiracy theories compelling to so many people? And why are some people more compelled to believe them than others?

Dozens of studies have begun to investigate these questions. Based on these studies, we know that people who believe in one conspiracy theory (say, that JFK was assassinated by the CIA) are also more likely to believe in others (for instance, that the moon landing was faked). In fact, people who endorse some conspiratorial claims (e.g., that Princess Diana faked her own death) are also

©2016 National Public Radio, Inc. NPR report titled "Is Education Tied To Conspiracy Theory Belief?" by Tania Lombrozo was originally published at NPR's 13.7: Cosmos & Culture on December 5, 2016, and is used with the permission of NPR. Any unauthorized duplication is strictly prohibited.

more likely to endorse inconsistent alternatives (e.g., that Princess Diana was murdered). These findings suggest that in addition to the idiosyncratic factors that figure into people's reasoning about each unique conspiracy theory, there are more general characteristics about some individuals or their environment that make them more or less inclined towards conspiratorial thinking.

What might these more general characteristics be?

Among other things, studies find that people are more likely to endorse conspiracy theories if they feel alienated, powerless and disadvantaged, and if they are distrustful of others. Conspiratorial thinking is also associated with narcissism, rejection of climate science, and an individual's own willingness to participate in conspiracies. Additionally, a variety of demographic factors have been found to predict conspiratorial thinking, including low levels of education.

These patterns of association are informative, but they're often difficult to interpret. For example, is it the case that education reduces belief in conspiracy theories, or that people who endorse conspiracy theories are less likely to pursue formal education? Moving from correlation to causation is difficult in such cases because a true experiment—in which, for example, people are randomly assigned to education levels—can be impossible, impractical or unethical.

Despite these challenges, two new papers shed light on the connection between education and conspiratorial thinking. They do so not by manipulating education experimentally, but by testing hypotheses about why and how education could affect belief in conspiracy theories. Specifically, the papers identify factors that mediate the relationship between education and conspiratorial thinking.

The first paper, authored by psychologist Karen Douglas and colleagues, was published earlier this year in the journal *Thinking & Reasoning*. It reports evidence that one factor mediating the relationship between lower education and conspiratorial thinking is the tendency to attribute agency and intentionality where it doesn't belong.

In two studies with more 500 participants who completed an online survey, people reported the extent to which they thought nonhuman animals (such as fish), natural entities (such as the ocean), and technological devices (such as televisions) possess attributes that are often restricted to humans, such as having intentions and free will. Those with higher education were less likely to extend these attributes beyond humans, while those who believed in conspiracy theories were more likely to do so. Most importantly, the relationship between education and conspiratorial beliefs could be explained in part by the association between each of these factors and the tendency to ascribe human attributes to non-humans. This suggests that education reduces over-attribution of agency and intentionality, and that this reduction decreases the appeal of conspiracy theories, which often posit one or more agents behind a constellation of potentially unrelated events.

The second paper, authored by psychologist Jan-Willem van Prooijen and forthcoming in the journal *Applied Cognitive Psychology*, finds support for two additional mediating factors: skepticism towards the idea that complex problems can have simple solutions, and greater feelings of control.

Across two samples of Dutch participants (one including 4,062 readers of a Dutch popular science magazine and the second a group of 1,251 adults selected to be representative of the Dutch population), participants with higher levels of education were more likely to disagree with statements suggesting simple solutions to complex problems, such as: "With the right policies, most problems in society are easy to solve." Participants with higher levels of education also felt that they had greater control over their political environment—they were less likely to report feeling powerless when watching how events unfold in the news, and more likely to agree with a statement such as: "Citizens can influence government decisions;" or "It is possible to object against government decisions." Most importantly, both of these factors also predicted skepticism towards conspiracy theories, with further analyses suggesting that the association between education and conspiratorial thinking was mediated by both of these factors.

While these papers fall short of establishing a causal connection between education and skepticism towards conspiracy theories, they point to the idea that education brings with it a suite of cognitive and affective consequences, and that these consequences can disrupt the processes that draw people towards conspiratorial beliefs in the first place. Moreover, they suggest that one of these cognitive consequences is a shift away from relatively intuitive and automatic processes—of the kind that support simple, intentional narratives—in favor of more deliberative, analytic thinking. In fact, the causal link between analytic thinking and greater rejection of conspiracy theories is the one piece of the story that does have direct experimental support: A paper published in 2014 found that having people complete a task that increased analytic thinking in the short term led them to report lower belief in conspiracy theories when asked immediately after. Education could be a way to generate similar but longer-lasting effects.

Not all conspiracy theories are harmful. Some might promote a healthy skepticism, and some might even be true. But many do have negative personal and political consequences. For these reasons alone, it makes sense to track how and why conspiracy theories arise and gain traction. Yet blaming errant tweets or other forms of social media is just one part of the picture. The real culprit is the human mind—the machinery that generates conspiratorial narratives in the first place, and that guides each subsequent tweet, share, and like.

Fighting the Irrational Can Be Difficult

Phil Whitby

Phil Whitby is a senior developer at Livepoint Software Solutions Ltd.

Whether you think you are rational or irrational, you're right. Do you believe in the time-worn adage "The customer is always right" or "A fool and his money are soon separated." How about "Birds of a feather flock together"? If so, do you also believe "Opposites attract"?

Even if you believe none of these, you will have multiple core beliefs—or axioms—that you consider self-evidently true. How often do you question the validity of these axioms? "Birds of a feather flock together" and "Opposites attract" are contradictory, or are they loosely indicative of a more nuanced truth that needs clarification?

Conspiracy theorists are maddening because they appear to be rational in their justifications; their statements have an internal logic if you accept that the primary axiom, or the foundational truth which they believe is unshakeable. This is why it can be so difficult to convince them with what appears to be logical.

The truly worrying aspect is that—despite perceiving ourselves as rational beings—we all suffer from this type of malady to some degree, even if you do believe in the validity of the moon-landing, the oblate-spheroid earth shape, or vaccines.

How Much Is the Ball?

Consider the bat and ball problem:

> A bat and a ball together cost £1.10.
>
> The bat costs £1 more than the ball.
>
> How much is the ball?

"Conspiracy theories - rational behaviour emerging from irrational certainty?" by Phil Whitby, Livepoint Software Solutions Ltd., May 3, 2019. Reprinted by permission.

You have probably warily muttered '10p' to yourself. You know this is likely wrong, but your intuitive initial answer convinces you that it must be 10p. Now when I tell you it is wrong, what are your first assumptions? If you are thinking "It's a trick question or "It must be a riddle." You are following the exact path of a conspiracy theorist.

Gödel Help Us

Well, you are following them to a point: a conspiracy theorist will steadfastly refuse to revise the belief that their first intuitive answer must be true. Instead anything contradicting their intuitive belief must be side-stepped, as it would be more outlandish for that axiom to be wrong than any circuitous reasoning that justifies it.

An individual's ego-driven need for certain axioms to be true is universal. Atheist or theist, chemtrail-ist or contrail-ist, you are likely to be highly emotionally tied to the underlying beliefs which inform your viewpoint. It is almost impossible to convince someone that their axioms are flawed, because beneath the primary axiom is this meta-axiom of self-belief that is never addressed by logically deconstructing an argument about Obama's birth certificate, Sandy Hook as a false-flag, or lizard people.

> "I am the rational keeper and protector of sacred, esoteric knowledge"

This meta-axiom must be preserved at all costs, as it is the basis of all self-worth for the conspiracy theorist. A recent study demonstrated that conspiracy theorists would believe in a fabricated conspiracy if they heard that a small percentage of the general population believed it (<20%), but would be indifferent if it was generally believed by the population (>80%).

This may be the reason that we will never extinguish the tendency with de-platforming: there will always be a fresh conspiracy to take its place, and the thirst for conspiracy is not quenched by the validation of an existing one.

What Are You Certain Of?

According to philosopher Justin E. Smith, human beings are uniquely irrational rather than rational, and attempts to impose rationality in society results in a huge reaction of irrationality. He argues that the excellent results of rational thinking in mechanical engineering and science led to the modern idea of a human as a "sub-machine within a big machine of society," but that this weak analogy does not adequately frame human behaviour. Phenomena such as the halo effect, court judges being more harsh before lunch, and evidence that using science in an argument actually makes people more partisan all contribute to this perception, and possibly to a growing sense of anxiety about the future of humanity.

The counterpoint to all this bleakness is that we humans are successful by dint of our irrationality. It is impossible to be perfectly rational at all times even if your axioms are sensible, as all the myriad factual information is not available that could conceivably affect an outcome. If you refuse to contemplate taking action until all the facts are in, then there will never be any decisive action. Emotions play such a part in your decision-making process that any damage to the region of the brain associated with emotion leads to endless procrastination in the individual.

How does this relate to conspiracy theorists? Well, as discussed above conspiracy theorists most specious axiom is that they are one of the select few capable of true rationality. The key to unlocking their obsession may be in revealing the contextual advantage of irrationality itself, and the inevitability of both succumbing to it and succeeding by it. The ego-driven axiom of being the "rational keeper of sacred knowledge" may be undone by making the awareness of irrationality a quality to be brandished, just as the pursuit of perfect rationality has been in the past. If this can be marketed to individuals the same way the sage wise man/nerd-savant is marketed to teenage boys, then there may be hope.

The same applies to any beliefs about business: you may make decisions about your market, growth, or employees based on an axiomatic choice that you made years ago without revisiting in the present day. Just look at industries that tried to hold on to business models that were long defunct: the recording and film industry with streaming (who both saw it as a conspiracy by their customers, and had them arrested), the camera film industry with digital sensors (kodak invented the first digital camera, then suppressed it). Axioms may be self-evidently true at one time, but you are not the sole arbiter of the persistence of that truth, and you are not entitled to be magically informed any time that changes.

I cannot be certain, of course: the ball may actually be 10p, and to think otherwise is just what 'Big Supermarket' *wants* you to think.

Inequality Plays a Role in the Spread of Conspiracy Theories

University of Cambridge

The University of Cambridge is a public research university in the United Kingdom.

The largest cross-national study ever conducted on conspiracy theories suggests that around a third of people in countries such as the UK and France think their governments are "hiding the truth" about immigration, and that voting for Brexit and Trump is associated with a wide range of conspiratorial beliefs—from science denial to takeover plots by Muslim migrants.

The research, conducted as part of the University of Cambridge's Conspiracy & Democracy project, and based on survey work from the YouGov-Cambridge centre, covers nine countries—US, Britain*, Poland, Italy, France, Germany, Portugal, Sweden, Hungary—and will be presented at a public launch in Cambridge on Friday 23 November.

According to project researcher Dr Hugo Leal, anti-immigration conspiracy theories have been "gaining ground" since the refugee crisis first came to prominence in 2015. "The conspiratorial perception that governments are deliberately hiding the truth about levels of migration appears to be backed by a considerable portion of the population across much of Europe and the United States," he said.

In Hungary, where controversial Prime Minister Viktor Orban is regularly accused of stoking anti-migrant sentiment, almost half of respondents (48%) believe their government is hiding the truth about immigration. Germany was the next highest (35%), with France (32%), Britain (30%) and Sweden (29%) also showing

"Brexit and Trump voters more likely to believe in conspiracy theories, study shows," University of Cambridge, November 23, 2018, https://www.cam.ac.uk/research/news/brexit-and-trump-voters-more-likely-to-believe-in-conspiracy-theories-survey-study-shows. Licensed under CC BY-SA 3.0.

Can Conspiracy Theories Be Stopped?

high percentages of this conspiracy among respondents, as well as a fifth (21%) of those in the United States.

Close to half of respondents who voted for Brexit (47%) and Trump (44%) believe their government is hiding the truth about immigration, compared with just 14% of Remain voters and 12% of Clinton voters.

The researchers also set out to measure the extent of belief in a conspiracy theory known as 'the great replacement': the idea that Muslim immigration is part of a bigger plan to make Muslims the majority of a country's population.

"Originally formulated in French far-right circles, the widespread belief in a supposedly outlandish nativist conspiracy theory known as the 'great replacement' is an important marker and predictor of the Trump and Brexit votes," said Leal. Some 41% of Trump voters and 31% of Brexit voters subscribed to this theory, compared with 3% of Clinton voters and 6% of Remain voters.

Researchers also looked at a number of other popular conspiracy theories. Both Trump and Brexit voters were more likely to believe that climate change is a hoax, vaccines are harmful, and that a group of people "secretly control events and rule the world together." "We found the existence of a conspiratorial worldview linking both electorates," said Leal.

He describes the levels of science denial as an "alarming global trend." In general, researchers found the idea that climate change is a hoax to be far more captivating for right-wing respondents, while scepticism about vaccines was less determined by "ideological affiliation".

The view that "the truth about the harmful effects of vaccines is being deliberately hidden from the public" ranged from lows of 10% in Britain to a startling quarter of the population—some 26%—in France.

The conspiracy belief that a secret cabal "control events and rule the world together" varies significantly between European countries such as Portugal (42%) and Sweden (12%). Dr Hugo Drochon, also a researcher on the Leverhulme Trust-funded Conspiracy &

Democracy project, suggests this has "public policy implications, because there are structural issues at play here too."

"More unequal countries with a lower quality of democracy tend to display higher levels of belief in the world cabal, which suggests that conspiracy beliefs can also be addressed at a more 'macro' level," said Drochon.

The research team assessed the levels of "conspiracy scepticism" by looking at those who refuted every conspiratorial view in the study. Sweden had the healthiest levels of overall conspiracy scepticism, with 48% rejecting every conspiracy put to them. The UK also had a relatively strong 40% rejection of all conspiracies. Hungary had the lowest, with just 15% of people not taken in by any conspiracy theories.

Half of both Remain and Clinton voters were conspiracy sceptics, while 29% of Brexit voters and just 16% of Trump voters rejected all conspiracy theories.

The question of trust, and which professions the public see as trustworthy, was also investigated by researchers. Government and big business came out worst across all countries included in the study. Roughly three-quarters of respondents in Italy, Portugal, Poland, Hungary and Britain say they distrusted government ministers and company CEOs. Distrust of journalists, trade unionists, senior officials of the EU, and religious leaders are also high in all surveyed countries.

Trust in academics, however, was still relatively high, standing at 57% in the US and 64% in Britain. "We hope these findings can provide incentive for academics to reclaim a more active role in the public sphere, particularly when it comes to illuminating the differences between verifiable truths and demonstrable falsehoods," said Hugo Leal.

Apart from academics, only family and friends escape the general climate of distrust, with trust reaching levels between 80% and 90% in all countries. Leal argues that this might help explain the credibility assigned to "friend mediated" online social networks.

In all surveyed countries apart from Germany, about half the respondents got their news from social media, with Facebook the preferred platform followed by YouTube. Getting news from social media was less likely to be associated with complete scepticism of conspiracy theories—much less likely in countries such as the US and Italy.

Researchers found that consuming news from YouTube in particular was associated with the adoption of particular conspiratorial views, such as anti-vaccine beliefs in the US and climate change denial in Britain.

"A telling takeaway of the study is that conspiracy theories are, nowadays, mainstream rather than marginal beliefs," said Leal. "These findings provide important clues to understanding the popularity of populist and nationalist parties contesting elections across much of the western world."

The survey was conducted by YouGov during 13-23 August 2018, with a total sample size of 11,523 adults and results then weighted to be "representative of each market."

* *Northern Ireland was not included in the survey.*

Trusting in Intuition Encourages Belief in Conspiracy Theories

R. Kelly Garrett

R. Kelly Garrett is an associate professor of communication at the Ohio State University.

Have you ever thought to yourself, "I'll bet that's true," before you had all the facts? Most people probably have at some point.

Where people differ is in how often they do so. A 2016 survey that my colleague Brian Weeks and I conducted found that 50.3 percent of all Americans agreed with the statement "I trust my gut to tell me what's true and what's not." Some of those polled felt quite strongly about it: About one in seven (14.6 percent) strongly agreed, while one in 10 (10.2 percent) strongly disagreed.

In other words, there's a lot of variation in how Americans decide what to believe.

In research published in 2017, we were able to use the findings from this survey and two others to dig into the different approaches people take when deciding what's true.

We found some surprising differences between how people think about intuition and how they think about evidence. It turns out that how often someone trusts their intuition and how important they think it is to have evidence are two separate things. Both make a big difference in what we believe.

What we learned offers some hope for people's ability to tell truth from fiction, despite the fact that so many trust their gut.

How Beliefs Are Formed

Many incorrect beliefs have political foundations. They promote a policy, an ideology or one candidate over another.

"Should we worry that half of Americans trust their gut to tell them what's true?" by R. Kelly Garrett, the Conversation, September 27, 2017, https://theconversation.com/should-we-worry-that-half-of-americans-trust-their-gut-to-tell-them-whats-true-84259. Licensed under CC BY-ND 4.0 International.

People are susceptible to political misinformation because they tend to believe things that favor their side—even if it isn't grounded in data or science. There are numerous factors at play, from the influence of nonconscious emotions to the need to defend a group that the individual identifies with.

For these reasons, millions of Americans believe things that aren't true.

People reject the conclusions of scientists when they deny humans' role in promoting climate change, question the safety of genetically modified foods or refuse to have their children vaccinated.

They reject the assessments of fact checkers, incorrectly believing that President Obama was born outside the U.S. or that Russia successfully tampered with vote tallies in the 2016 presidential election. And certain conspiracy theories — like the belief that President Kennedy's assassination was orchestrated by a powerful secret organization—are remarkably persistent.

With all the talk about political bias, it's easy to lose track of the fact that politics aren't the only thing shaping people's beliefs. Other factors play a role too.

For example, people are more likely to believe something the more often they've heard it said—commonly known as the illusory truth effect. And adding a picture can change how believable a message is, sometimes making it more convincing, while at other times increasing skepticism.

Valuing Intuition Versus Valuing Evidence

Our study focuses on something else that shapes beliefs: We looked at what matters the most to people when they're deciding what's true.

We found that having faith in your intuition about the facts does make you more likely to endorse conspiracy theories. However, it doesn't really influence your beliefs about science, such as vaccine safety or climate change.

In contrast, someone who says beliefs must be supported with data is more likely both to reject conspiracy theories and to answer questions about mainstream science and political issues more accurately.

The risk of relying on one's intuition may be self-evident, but its role in belief formation is more nuanced.

Although our study shows that trusting gut feelings is associated with belief in conspiracy theories, this doesn't mean that intuition is always wrong. (Occasionally a conspiracy does turn out to be real.)

Furthermore, intuition isn't all bad. There's lots of evidence that a person who is unable to use feelings in forming a judgment tends to make very poor decisions.

In the end, knowing how much someone trusts his or her intuition actually tells you very little about how much proof that person will need before he or she will believe a claim. Our research shows that using intuition is not the opposite of checking the evidence: Some people trust their instincts while at the same time valuing evidence; others deny the importance of both; and so forth.

The key is that some people—even if they usually trust their gut—will check their hunches to make sure they're right. Their willingness to do some follow-up work may explain why their beliefs tend to be more accurate.

It's valuing evidence that predicts accuracy on a wider range of issues. Intuition matters less.

It's All About the Evidence

These findings might seem obvious. But researchers studying misperceptions often find that "obvious" predictors don't work the way we hope they would.

For example, one study sorted people based on how accurate they are when solving problems for which the obvious answer is incorrect: If a bat and a ball cost US$1.10 in total, and the bat costs $1.00 more than the ball, how much does the ball cost? (It's not $.10.) Results show that individuals who got questions similar to this one right tended to be more biased in their beliefs about climate change.

Another study found that people with the strongest reasoning skills and the highest science literacy also tend to be more biased in their interpretation of new information. Even asking people to "think carefully" can lead to more biased answers.

Can Conspiracy Theories Be Stopped?

In this context, our results are surprising. There are many individual qualities that seem like they should promote accuracy, but don't.

Valuing evidence, however, appears to be an exception. The bigger the role evidence plays in shaping a person's beliefs, the more accurate that person tends to be.

We aren't the only ones who have observed a pattern like this. Another recent study shows that people who exhibit higher scientific curiosity also tend to adopt more accurate beliefs about politically charged science topics, such as fracking and global warming.

There's more we need to understand. It isn't yet clear why curiosity and attention to the evidence leads to better outcomes, while being knowledgeable and thinking carefully promote bias. Until we sort this out, it's hard to know exactly what kinds of media literacy skills will help the most.

But in today's media environment—where news consumers are subjected to a barrage of opinions, data and misinformation—gut feelings and people's need for evidence to back those hunches up can play a big role. They might determine whether you fall for a hoax posted on the Onion, help spread Russian disinformation or believe that the British spy agency MI6 was responsible for Princess Diana's death.

For now, though, when it comes to fighting the scourge of misinformation, there's a simple strategy that everyone can use. If you are someone who consistently checks your intuition about what is true against the evidence, you are less likely to be misled. It may seem like common sense, but learning to dig into the story behind that shocking headline can help you avoid spreading falsehoods.

So if someone shares something with you that you know is false—especially if it is someone you know—don't be afraid to disagree.

There's no need for name calling; studies have shown that just providing evidence can make a difference, if not for the person who shared the falsehood, then at least for others who were exposed to it.

In a world where the very idea of "truth" often appears under attack, this is an easy way that individuals can make a difference.

Organizations to Contact

The editors have compiled the following list of organizations concerned with the issues debated in this book. The descriptions are derived from materials provided by the organizations. All have publications or information available for interested readers. This list was compiled on the date of publication of the present volume; the information provided here may change. Be aware that many organizations take several weeks or longer to respond to inquiries, so allow as much time as possible.

American Civil Liberties Union (ACLU)
125 Broad Street, 18th Floor
New York, NY 10004
phone: (212) 549-2500
email: info@acludc.org
website: www.aclu.org

The ACLU is a long-running civil rights organization that advocates for Constitutional liberties and uses the courts to help those whose rights may have been infringed upon. The group works on both a national and regional level, and most states or cities have a local branch that can be contacted.

Defending Rights and Dissent
1325 G Street NW, Suite 500
Washington, DC 20005
phone: (202) 552-7408
email: info@rightsanddissent.org
website: www.rightsanddissent.org

This nonprofit organization focuses on advocating for the freedom of political expression, as well as the rights outlined in the Bill of Rights more broadly. Their work includes government and law enforcement accountability, training, and information gathering.

First Amendment Center
555 Pennsylvania Avenue NW
Washington, DC 20001
phone: (202) 292-6290
email: firstamendmentcenter@newseum.org
website: www.freedomforuminstitute.org

Housed at the Freedom Forum Institute, the First Amendment Center works to raise public awareness and knowledge about the First Amendment rights, including freedom of speech and freedom of the press. Their website features resources like interactive tools to help teach what is and is not misinformation, surveys, and publications.

Foundation for Individual Rights in Education (FIRE)
510 Walnut Street, Suite 1250
Philadelphia, PA 19106
phone: (215) 717-FIRE
email: fire@thefire.org
website: www.thefire.org

This free speech organization focuses on protecting the First Amendment on college campuses. The group provides resources and support to faculty and students who feel their civil liberties may have been violated, and works to reform university policies to protect free speech.

Institute for Free Speech
124 S. West Street, Suite 201
Alexandria, VA 22314
phone: (703) 894-6800
website: www.ifs.org

This organization uses litigation, research, publishing, and educational initiatives to raise awareness of and protect the First Amendment, particularly the right to free speech. The group draws attention to and challenges laws that could violate free speech at a state and local level.

Knight First Amendment Institute
475 Riverside Drive, Suite 302
New York, NY 10115
phone: (646) 745-8500
email: info@knightcolumbia.org
website: www.knightcolumbia.org

Housed at Columbia University, the Knight First Amendment Institute advocates for the freedom of the press and freedom of speech. The organization brings lawsuits against prominent government figures and agencies. It also publishes resources on a range of topics related to their area of focus.

National Freedom of Information Coalition (NFOIC)
3208 Weimar Hall
PO Box 118400
Gainesville, FL 32611-8400
phone: (352) 294-7082
email: nfoic@nfoic.org
website: nfoic.org

Housed at the University of Florida's College of Journalism and Communications, NFOIC focuses on government transparency and accountability. Working at a national and local level, the organization provides resources for those pursuing open records, training, and assistance with litigation regarding transparency.

Southern Poverty Law Center (SPLC)
400 Washington Avenue
Montgomery, AL 36104
phone: (334) 956-8200
website: www.splcenter.org

The SPLC is a leading research and advocacy group working to raise awareness of hate groups and extremism in the United States. The group provides resources that include tools to track hate groups and reports. The group also brings litigation related to their areas of focus, as well as equality and justice more broadly.

United States Holocaust Museum
100 Raoul Wallenberg Pl SW
Washington, DC 20024
phone: (202) 488-0400
website: www.ushmm.org

This DC-based museum serves to educate the public on the Holocaust, genocide, and anti-Semitism. The museum's website features resources on these topics, as well as memorials to the victims of the Holocaust.

World Jewish Restitution Organization (WJRO)
5 Mapu St
Jerusalem 94189
Israel
phone: +972-2-5612497
website: wjro.org.il

WJRO focuses on raising awareness of and securing restitution for Jewish victims of the Holocaust. The group also publishes information on the impact of the Holocaust, reports, and international resolutions.

Bibliography

Books

William J. Birnes and Philip Corso. *The Day After Roswell.* New York, NY: Atria Books, 1999.

Rob Brotherton. *Suspicious Minds.* New York, NY: Bloomsbury, 2015.

Lance deHaven-Smith. *Conspiracy Theory in America.* Austin, TX: University of Texas Press, 2013.

Brian Dunning. *Conspiracies Declassified.* Avon, MA: Adams Media, 2018

Jonathan Haidt. *The Righteous Mind.* New York, NY: Vintage, 2013.

Deborah E. Lipstadt. *History on Trial: My Day in Court with a Holocaust Denier.* New York, NY: Harper Perennial, 2006.

Anna Merlan. *Republic of Lies.* New York, NY: Macmillan, 2019.

Steven Novella, Cara Santa Maria, Jay Novella, Bob Novella, and Evan Bernstein. *The Skeptic's Guide to the Universe.* New York, NY: Grand Central Publishing, 2018.

Caitlin O'Connor and James Owen Weatherball. *The Misinformation Age: How False Beliefs Spread.* Hartford, CT: Yale University Press, 2018.

Nancy L. Rosenblum and Russell Muirhead. *A Lot of People Are Saying.* Princeton, NJ: Princeton University Press, 2019.

Michael Shermer. *Skeptic.* New York, NY: St Martin's Griffin, 2017.

Justin E. H. Smith. *Irrationality.* Princeton, NJ: Princeton University Press, 2019.

Frank Snepp. *Irreparable Harm.* Lawrence, KS: University Press of Kansas, 2001

Jan-Willem van Prooijen. *The Psychology of Conspiracy Theories.* Abingdon, UK: Routledge, 2018.

Jesse Walker. *The United States of Paranoia.* New York, NY: Harper, 2013

Periodicals and Internet Sources

Sean Illing. "The Trump-Ukraine story shows the power of conspiracy theories," *Vox,* October 1, 2019. https://www.vox.com/2019/4/11/18291061/trump-ukraine-barr-whistleblower-investigation.

Jarek Keller, "Is A Conspiracy Theory Protected Speech?" *Pacific Standard,* August 6, 2019. https://psmag.com/social-justice/is-a-conspiracy-theory-protected-speech.

Stephan Lewandowsky. "A new tool can help us determine which conspiracy theories are false and which might be true," LSE US Centre, January 4, 2019. https://blogs.lse.ac.uk/usappblog/2019/01/04/a-new-tool-can-help-us-determine-which-conspiracy-theories-are-false-and-which-might-be-true/.

Earl Meagan. "Why Do People Believe in Conspiracy Theories?" *BrainWorld,* April 4, 2019. https://brainworldmagazine.com/people-believe-conspiracy-theories/.

Russell Muirhead and Nancy Rosenblum, "The New Conspiracists," *Dissent,* Winter 2018. https://www.dissentmagazine.org/article/conspiracy-theories-politics-infowars-threat-democracy.

Marius H. Raab, Stefan A. Ortlieb, Nikolas Auer, Klara Guthmann, and Claus-Christian Carbon, "Thirty shades of truth: conspiracy theories as stories of individuation, not of pathological delusion," *Frontiers in Psychology,* July

9, 2013. https://www.frontiersin.org/articles/10.3389/fpsyg.2013.00406/full.

Ivana Rihter, "Why Believing Conspiracy Theories Feels So Good," the *Outline*, March 28, 2018. https://theoutline.com/post/3959/conspiracy-theories-psychology-lizard-people-crisis-actor-birtherism?zd=1&zi=7edxhqdq.

Roger W. Smith, "Legislating against Genocide Denial: Criminalizing Denial or Preventing Free Speech?" *University of St. Thomas Journal of Law and Public Policy*, Spring 2010. https://ir.stthomas.edu/cgi/viewcontent.cgi?article=1050&context=ustjlpp.

Piia Varis, "Conspiracy theorising online," *Diggit Magazine*, October 11, 2019. https://www.diggitmagazine.com/articles/conspiracy-theorising-online.

Kelly Weill, "How YouTube Built a Radicalization Machine for the Far-Right," the *Daily Beast*, December 17, 2018. https://www.thedailybeast.com/how-youtube-pulled-these-men-down-a-vortex-of-far-right-hate.

Index

A

Aldrin, Buzz, 75
Ali, Jason Mostafa, 132–135
American Conspiracy Theories, 58
Apollo Simulation Project, 75
Area 51, 14, 73
Armijo, Enrique, 144–147
Armstrong, Neil, 49, 50, 75
Ash, Timothy Garton, 98–101
Assange, Julian, 83
autism, 30

B

Barnes, Luke, 24–27
bat and ball problem, 152–153
Bilfield, Jeremy, 117–124
Black Lives Matter, 36, 83
Boston Marathon Bombing, 33, 82
Brandon, Lewis, 87, 88
Bush, George W., 84

C

Cali, Francesco, 25
Callaghan, Timothy, 28–32
Carto, Willis, 87, 88
Cherry, Kendra, 137–143
climate change, 80, 157, 159, 161

Clinton, Bill, 24, 27, 81, 83
Clinton, Hillary, 22, 24, 27, 57, 83, 158
Cohnitz, Daniel, 41–48
Collins, Michael, 75
Comet Ping Pong, 21, 25
Comey, James, 22
conspiracy theories, history of, 14–15, 18–20, 78–80, 81–84
crisis actors, 33–36, 145
Cruz, Ted, 62, 81

D

Daily Stormer, 71, 72, 117
Dallas police shooting, 36
Deep State, 18, 24, 25, 37
disconfirmation bias, 65
domestic terrorism, conspiracy theories as impetus for, 15, 24–27
Douglas, Karen, 78–80, 149
Duke, David, 88
Dunning, David, 62–65

E

education level, and belief in conspiracy theories, 148–151
8chan, 24

171

F

Facebook, 34, 60, 63, 66, 84, 125–131, 159
false flags, 22, 24, 33, 36, 82, 153
Federal Bureau of Investigation, 21–23, 24–27, 83
Feynman, Richard, 52–53
First Amendment, 23, 105–107, 134, 144–147
4chan, 15, 22, 24, 34, 67, 71

G

Gab, 66
Gaetz, Matt, 67
Garrett, R. Kelly, 160–163
Gateway Pundit, 34
German, Michael, 23
Germany, criminalization of Holocaust denial in, 98–101, 108–109, 110–112, 113–116, 126
Greene, David, 66–69
Greenville rally, 22

H

Hart, Joshua, 37–40
Haven, Lisa, 34
health care, conspiracy theories about, 15, 28–32, 53, 80, 82, 83, 157, 159
Heideman, Elana, 125–131
Heinze, Eric, 110–112
Hilberg, Raul, 91, 92

Holocaust denial, 14, 15, 70–72, 86–97, 98–101, 102–109, 110–112, 113–116, 117–124, 125–131, 132–135
Honduras, and migrant caravan, 67
Hoover Dam, 21, 25

I

Illuminati, 14
Imperium—The Philosophy of History and Politics, 88
inequality, and susceptibility to belief in conspiracy theories, 156–159
Information Disorder Lab Team, 33–36
Info Wars, 59, 144
Institute for Historical Review (IHR), 71, 87–88
intuition, as opposed to reason in forming beliefs, 160–163
Iran-Contra affair, 143
Irma, Hurricane, 84
Irving, David, 71, 89, 99, 113–114, 115, 132

J

Joint Council for Repatriation, 88
Jones, Alex, 22, 38, 59, 81, 82, 84, 144–147
Journal for Historical Review, 87

K

Katrina, Hurricane, 83
Kaysing, Bill, 33, 74, 76
Kennedy, John F.,
    assassination of, 14, 29,
    58–59, 81, 148, 161
Kennedy, Robert F., Jr., 82
King, Martin Luther, Jr., 83
Kruger, Justin, 64
Kubrick, Stanley, 50, 75
Ku Klux Klan, 88

L

Lasson, Kenneth, 102–109
Last Skeptic of Science, The, 76
Lewis, Bernard, 108
Liberty Lobby, 87
Limbaugh, Rush, 84
Lipstadt, Deborah, 89, 94, 99,
    114, 117, 118, 119, 120,
    121, 122, 132
Lombrozo, Tania, 148–151
Lorch, Mark, 49–55
lunar landing, conspiracy
    theories surrounding, 14,
    29, 49–50, 73–77

M

Manchester bombing, 82
Marcellus, Tom, 87, 88
Maria, Hurricane, 81
Mather, Cotton, 81
measles, 15, 28–32
memory laws, 110, 112

Mendelsohn, John, 91
Merlan, Anna, 81–84
migrant caravan, 36, 67
Milgram, Stanley, 51
Miller, Scott, 86–97
Motta, Matt, 28–32
Mulhall, Joe, 70–72

N

NASA Mooned America!, 76
National Association for the
    Advancement of White
    People, 88
National Basketball
    Association, 62
National Front, 88, 99
National Security Agency, 41
Novak, Matt, 73–77

O

Obama, Barack, 19, 35, 36, 37,
    60, 81, 144, 148, 153, 161
Oklahoma City bombing, 82
Oswald, Lee Harvey, 29

P

Paltrow, Gwyneth, 49
"Paranoid Style in American
    Politics, The," 82
Parent, Joseph, 19, 58
peer pressure, role in believing
    conspiracy theories, 51–53
Peinovich, Mike, 72
Pence, Michael, 81

Pizzagate, 18, 21, 24, 25, 72, 143
political extremism, conspiracy theories as source of, 15, 21–23, 24–27
psychological profile, of conspiracy theorists, 37–40, 49–55, 137–143
Pulse nightclub shooting, 33

Q

QAnon, 21, 22, 24–27, 40, 82

R

Reddit, 35, 67
Rene, Ralph, 75–76
Republic of Lies, 81–84
Rich, Jennifer, 132–135
Rich, Seth, 82, 83
ruling class, conspiracy theories as criticism of, 41–48

S

Sanchez, Brandon, 81–84
Sandy Hook Elementary shooting, 22, 33, 82, 144–147, 153
Scalia, Antonin, 60
schizotypy, 38
September 11, 2001, terrorist attacks (9/11), 19, 36, 41, 79, 134, 135
Smith, Justin E., 154
Snoop Dog, 83

Snowden, Edward, 41
Social Science's Conspiracy-Theory Panic: Now They Want to Cure Everyone, 42

T

Tree of Life synagogue shooting, 21
Trump, Donald, 18, 21, 22, 24, 35, 36, 37, 39, 40, 49, 57, 67, 81, 83, 84, 157, 158
"Truth Behind the Moon Landings, The," 76
Tuskegee experiments, 143
Twitter, 25, 27, 34, 35, 36, 50, 60, 66, 81
2001: A Space Odyssey, 75

U

United States Holocaust Memorial Museum, 93–94, 102, 104
University of Cambridge, 156–159
Uscinski, Joe, 19, 57–61

V

vaccines, conspiracy theories concerning, 15, 28–32, 53, 80, 82, 83, 157, 159
van Prooijen, Jan-Willem, 150
Veterans on Patrol, 22
View, Travis, 25–27
Vittert, Liberty, 18–20

W

Wagener, Volker, 113–116
Watergate, 40, 73
Weber, Mark, 87, 88
Wells Fargo, 84
We Never Went to the Moon, 73
Wexner Learning Center, 93
Wheeler, Rod, 83
Whitby, Phil, 152–155
Williams, Elanor, 64
Williamson, Richard, 114–115
Wilson, Jason, 21–23

Y

Yockey, Francis Parker, 88
YouTube, 34, 63, 74, 76, 81, 159

Z

Zappa, Frank, 110
Zundel, Ernst, 89